CHAPTER 1

In the Headlights

VAGGGHHHRRRROOOOOOOOOM! Milo Fisher flew back in his seat as his father floored the accelerator. The boorish rev of the cobalt blue sports car echoed across the Dentalia mountains.

Mr Fisher switched gears and they zipped round a bend, dissipating wavy columns of mist rising from rust-coloured leaves blanketing the forest floor.

"What did I tell you about the cornering on this machine?" Fisher flashed his son a toothy grin as they continued down the deserted dirt road winding through Nu Co.'s vast forested property. "Have you ever felt so alive?"

Milo swallowed the sick creeping up the back of his throat. *I wonder how alive Dad would feel if I vomited grapefruit juice and poached eggs all over his ridiculous new car?* "This is great," he said, trying to sound cheerful rather than terrified. He gripped the edge of his seat as they raced down a steep incline.

Mr Fisher had purchased the Aston Martin to celebrate the launch of his company's latest moneymaking venture. After the public relations disaster caused by Nucralose, a pine-sap sweetener that turned out to have some rather unfortunate side effects on the local populace, Fisher was "pivoting" Nu Co. in a fresh direction. All Milo knew about the endeavour was that it was keeping his father extremely busy. So busy that he'd cancelled their trip to Vancouver for a wildlife photography exhibition that Milo had set his heart on. *Figures*.

As a consolation prize, Fisher had woken his son before dawn for a surprise ride in the flashy two-seater. "Driving a fast car down an open road is as American as apple pie," Fisher winked.

Aren't these things made in England?

Milo stared out the window. A flock of crows took off cacophonously from a tangle of naked branches as the coupé zoomed past, forming a speckled swirl of darkness across the pink clouds.

If only I could fly away, too.

The sun peeked over the jagged mountains, illuminating a landscape scarred by recent deforestation. Nu Co. was in the midst of expanding its operations in Sticky Pines.

"Could you slow down a bit?" Milo rolled down the window.

"Where's the fun in that?" Fisher scoffed.

"I'm starting to feel carsick."

Mr Fisher slowed the vehicle. "That better?"

Milo offered a feeble thumbs-up. This was the first "quality time" he and his father had shared in over a month. He'd always enjoyed their special outings, but lately things between them had been ... complicated.

The strange events that had transpired several weeks ago skipped through Milo's mind in flashes of sticky golden goo, hideous hairy beasts, and the determined face of a girl with glasses and purple hair – a face he tried not to think about these days.

Mr Fisher braked hard in front of a hiking trail. "Think we can fit through there, sport?" With a glint in his eye, he trundled the compact car on to the footpath. They drove through a grove of indigo-needled pines, their twisty grey trunks glistening with the unique black sap from which Nu Co.'s products were made.

Is Dad showing off or what? "Aren't you supposed to stay on the road?" Milo stuffed his hands into the pockets of his black pea coat.

Mr Fisher reached over and mussed his son's sandy brown hair. "This is private property, kid. The rules don't apply here. And besides," he added, "this forest won't be here for much longer. Consider this a farewell tour."

Milo looked around the dappled hillside. "Do

you really have to cut it all down?"

"Nothing lasts forever," said Fisher. "Sticky pine sap is worth its weight in gold. The stuff can be used in construction, medicine, technology, you name it. What's a few trees, compared to all that?"

Fisher checked the time on his wrist, where he was wearing two different watches. One was his usual platinum Rolex, but he'd recently been sporting a black digital device as well. Instead of telling time, it displayed a high-security password that changed every thirty seconds. Milo didn't know what it was for.

"I suppose you have to go to work soon?" said Milo.

"I'm afraid so."

If Dad couldn't take me to the photography exhibition, he could at least have taken half a day off. "I'd better get to school, then."

Milo slumped in his seat. School was an emotional minefield these days. He'd started eating lunch in the debate classroom so he no longer had to run into his former friends Lucy Sladan and Tex Arkhipov. Which was fine. He didn't need them. He had a very respectable array of acquaintances. Acquaintances who, sure, were maybe not as interesting, fiery or funny as Lucy and Tex, but who were much more compatible with Milo's goals and interests. "Popular", "sporty", "fashionable" acquaintances, who didn't suddenly stop caring about their supposed principles and betray his trust when he stuck his neck out on the line for them.

"Ah, there it is." Mr Fisher steered the coupé off the dirt trail. "We just finished the road up here."

Bumping over a patch of purple ferns, they exited on to a stretch of fresh asphalt that meandered along the edge of a ridge overlooking Black Hole Lake – the always steaming, near-perfect circle of deep, murky water at the centre of the Big Crater Valley.

"Tell you what," said Fisher, accelerating

up the smooth roadway. "Why don't you skip school and hang out here, by the lake? I can have Kaitlyn bring over the jet ski."

"It's freezing out," said Milo. "You'd have to be crazy to go on the water right now."

That sounds like one of Lucy's insane ideas. Milo smirked as he remembered the peculiar girl running fearlessly through the woods, violet hair flying, chasing an honest-to-goodness monster. His smile faded as he remembered where she'd ended up that day: on the cold factory floor, his father's hands around her throat.

"Then tell me," said Fisher. "What do you plan to do today?" He kicked the car into high gear, leaning into a corner that was perilously close to the ledge.

Milo grimaced. "Just take me home. I'll watch a movie or something."

"You've been sulking indoors for over a month," said Fisher. "It's not healthy."

"Someone's throwing a Halloween party in town," said Milo. "Maybe you could drop me off this evening?"

"I have to work late." Fisher gripped the wheel. "Your stepmother can take you."

"I see." Milo crossed his arms.

Fisher turned to his son. "Look," he said, "I'm sorry I've been so busy lately, but you have to understand, it's—"

BAM!

There was a massive bump as the car collided with something big. Milo felt the shock of the impact through his bones. The car lost control and veered towards the cliff, the view from the windscreen rapidly filling up with sky.

"Son of a—" Fisher frantically steered the fishtailing automobile away from the precipice, but he overcorrected and they spun out of control.

Milo screamed as they reeled into the open forest and then, with a horrendous CRUNCH, slammed sideways into a tree, airbags deploying on all sides.

Smoke drifted out from under the hood of the

car and the engine was making an unsettling popping sound.

Groaning, Fisher switched off the motor and unbuckled his seat belt. He stretched his neck stiffly from side to side, but appeared largely unharmed.

Milo's head felt fuzzy, his heart pounding in his ears. The accident had seemed to happen both instantaneously and in slow motion. The air smelled of rubber and his cheek felt as if it had been burned. When he moved, bits of broken glass from the shattered passenger window fell from his lapel like small chunks of ice.

"Are you all right?" asked Fisher.

Good question. Milo fumbled with the vanity mirror. The right side of his face was red from where it hit the airbag, but he didn't see any blood. "I think I'm okay." He took a deep breath to slow his pulse. "What happened?"

A look of horror washed over Fisher's face. "The Aston Martin." He peeled himself out of the vehicle to assess the damage.

Milo's door was pinned against the trunk of a surprisingly sturdy tree. Pushing the flabby airbags out of his way, he climbed out the driver's side door after his father.

Mr Fisher surveyed the scene, his hands buried in his buoyant salt-and-pepper hair. The small automobile had collided with a burly oak. Its right front wheel was propped up on a massive gnarled root that stuck out of the soil like a bony knuckle.

Milo rotated his smarting right shoulder. "Do you think it's totalled?"

"No." Fisher's jaw was set. "Anything can be fixed with enough determination."

Milo walked round to the front of the car. There was a big dent in the hood. "Dad, what did we hit?"

"Stupid deer," Fisher muttered. He bent low to check the wheels. "Came from nowhere."

"You hit a deer?" said Milo, aghast. "Where is it?" He looked back towards the road for the injured animal, but couldn't see anything.

Maybe it fell over the edge? His throat felt tight.

"That dumb animal hit *us*," Fisher barked.

"I told you you were driving too fast!" Milo raced down the road and peered over the ridge, scanning the steep slope that ended at the lake's shore. *Where did it go?* His breath formed a smoke signal of distress in the cold October air.

At last, he spotted something. There, about fifty metres down, a white stag lay at the foot of a boulder. It didn't appear to be moving, at first, but then Milo saw it lift its head.

"I see the deer," he called to his father. "It's hurt, but alive!"

"Leave it alone," said Fisher, typing on his mobile. "Injured animals are dangerous. There's nothing we can do, anyway."

I thought anything could be fixed with enough determination? "We have to help it," Milo insisted.

Carefully, he picked his way down the embankment, sending loose veins of dirt crumbling down the slope. When he reached the bottom, he slowed his pace to approach the fallen deer. It was much bigger than it appeared from above, nearly the size of a horse. Milo was struck by its unusual, ghostly beauty.

The animal was breathing heavily and its forelimbs were bent at an odd angle. *Its legs could be broken.* As he approached, Milo was increasingly aware of the stag's formidable antlers. They'd need to get the poor thing to a veterinarian, but how?

"I'm not going to hurt you," said Milo, taking a step nearer.

Abruptly, the stag scrambled to its feet, snorting plumes of hot air into the cold wind.

Milo stumbled backwards and fell on to the gravel. The immense animal took a clumsy step towards him, its knees shaking. For a moment, the boy and the deer watched each other warily.

Then Milo broke into a grin. "You can walk," he said. The stag cocked its head, its ivory antlers catching a ray of sunlight.

"What are you doing?" Mr Fisher's voice boomed down the hillside. "I told you, that animal is dangerous!"

Milo looked up at his father who was peering down from the road. "Dad, wait, you'll scare it!"

But it was too late. Fisher was already barrelling down the slope. "Get away! GO!" he shouted, waving his arms.

Panicking, the deer reared and staggered across the shallow beach towards the water's edge.

Mr Fisher slid to the base of the hill and helped Milo to his feet. "What happened?" he asked. "Did it charge at you?"

"No, I'm fine." Milo glanced back to see the animal plunging into the lake. *Oh no. Deer can't swim, can they?*

Father and son watched as the stag swam out towards the centre of the broad body of water. It appeared to be heading for a small mist-shrouded island about as big as the Fisher family's eight-bedroom lodge.

That island's too far away. Milo's heart sank. *It*

will never make it!

His worries were justified. After a minute, the stag appeared to be in distress, its head dipping under the water again and again. Was it simply struggling to swim? To Milo, it almost looked like something was trying to pull it under...

Hands behind his head, Milo watched as the animal's magnificent pale antlers suddenly disappeared into the deep, leaving nothing but a faint swell on the inky water.

It did not resurface.

Milo released the breath he'd been holding. It was gone. There was nothing he could do.

Mr Fisher cleared his throat. "It wouldn't have survived anyway, son," he said, gently. "That's just the way of the world. These things happen."

But it only happened because you crashed into it.

"I think we should make a donation to a wildlife sanctuary in its honour," said Milo.

Fisher chuckled. "Sure." He pulled his son close. "I was a bit of a hippy at your age, too. Don't worry, you'll grow out of it." He gave him a squeeze. "It's you and me, kid. Us against the world. Same as always."

"Right," Milo replied. "Same as always."

Is it, though?

They stood quietly as the rising sun slowly burned the morning mist off the lake. Briefly, Milo thought he saw a large dark shape under the water's surface where the stag had disappeared. It was too big to be the deer, though. *Must be the shadow of a cloud…*

"Come on," said Fisher. "Murl will be here any minute with a tow truck. Shall we get you home?"

"Just take me to school."

"You sure?" said Fisher.

"No," said Milo. "I'm not." Without another word, he trudged back up the ridge, gripping fistfuls of dirt as he climbed.

Fisher followed close behind, keeping his hands free in case his son slipped.

Behind them, off in the distance, a songbird darted over the water, then dipped down to pluck a floating insect. In a flash, a dark, slimy tentacle emerged from the murky depths. It gripped the bird and hungrily snapped it underwater, leaving nothing but a flutter of loose feathers on the steamy surface of Black Hole Lake.

CHAPTER 2

Party Pooper

"*NuqneH!*" Tex greeted Lucy in Klingon from his front door. He pounded the plastic chain-link sash across his chest.

His forehead was covered in a ridged prosthetic complete with a black ponytailed wig. He wore a set of snaggly yellowish fake teeth that made him talk funny. It was an impressively detailed Halloween costume.

"Live long and prosper." Lucy held out her hand, her fingers splayed uncomfortably in the classic *Star Trek* "V". With her other hand, she scratched the latex folds on the bridge of her nose. Her mother had moulded and painted the piece, then glued it to Lucy's face for the evening's festivities. Lucy's purple hair was slicked back, secured with a thick orange headband that matched her sweater.

Tex shook his head. "That is what Vulcans say. You do not look like a Vulcan, Lucille."

"I'm a Bajoran." Lucy shook the dangling jewelled earring on her left ear. "Obviously."

"What do Bajorans say?"

"Let me in or I'll lead an insurrection against your house?"

Tex stepped aside and gestured for her to enter. The crackle of frying pierogi welcomed Lucy to the Arkhipov household.

After dinner, they planned to head two houses down to the Halloween party at Joey Peluso's place. Joey was a star soccer player and one of the most popular kids in Lucy's grade. They ran in different social circles, which may as well be different planets. Getting an invite to his party was one of the few perks of Lucy's mother being the school science teacher, in charge of grades and therefore destinies. Still, Lucy would have been happy to skip the party in favour of watching the latest horror flick at the cineplex. Except for one thing...

"Do you think Feesh will be at the party?" Tex asked wistfully as they entered the kitchen.

"Who? Milo Fisher?" Lucy scratched her head. "Why would I know?"

She did know. She had overheard Amy Overwhig talking to Jaimie Johnson about Milo in the girl's bathroom. Apparently, Amy thought he was the best-looking guy in school. *Not that it's a high bar. It's probably because he showers daily.*

"Do I smell onions?" Lucy said, taking a seat at the round kitchen table.

"Onions, cheese, potatoes and dough," said Tex's mother, Anna. She picked a few dumplings out of the pan and set them on a plate to cool. "All four major food groups for you, my dear."

"Lucita!" Tex's father Serge had just arrived home from work at the deli he ran downtown.

He slapped Lucy on the back, hard enough her glasses slid down her nose. "Long time no see, *kidushka.*" He pulled his trousers up over his belly and grabbed a steaming pierogi from the plate, juggling it from one hand to another before tossing it back. "Too hot," he winced.

Anna shooed him away and put the plate on the table for Lucy and Tex. "It is good to see you, Lucy dear. Where have you been hiding?"

Tex set his fake teeth on the floral tablecloth and dug into the food.

"Ummm..." Lucy reached for a pierogi.

What was there to say? *I've spent the last month trying to track down the members of a mysterious race of cryptozoological shapeshifters known as the Pretenders. They live hidden amongst the unsuspecting populace of Sticky Pines and are susceptible to the effects of Mr Fisher's sinister pine sweetener Nucralose. In order to protect them I can't reveal the Truth to anyone: not Tex, not my parents, not even Milo Fisher, who hates me because he doesn't understand why I had to lie about what we saw. I will remain in unrelenting agony until I solve the unfathomable mysteries of the universe. Can you please pass the ketchup?*

It was all true, of course. After Lucy had witnessed her English teacher, Mrs Stricks, and her wife transform into monkeyflippin' OWLS, she was left with nothing but questions. What were they? Aliens? Witches? Transdimensional shamanistic warriors? What did they want and how many of them were there?

Over the past few weeks, Lucy had been working alone to answer these questions. Unfortunately, Mrs Stricks had taken a sudden sabbatical, leaving a substitute teacher in charge of all her English classes. Neither she nor the Other Mrs Stricks would answer the door to their cabin, despite three straight hours of sustained knocking. Many of the other people Lucy hoped to investigate were inaccessible, mostly because she didn't know where they lived: Carlos Felina, the handsome weatherman, Steve Kozlowski, her father's bandmate, and Alastair Chelon, a factory worker. And then there was Mandy Millepoids, the owner of the local candy store. The last time Lucy had tried to enter Mandy's Candies, she'd encountered a locked door with a sign that read: "Pulling Taffy, Be Back in Ten Minutes". She waited for over two hours before giving up, going home and rage-screaming into her pillow.

"These are delicious, Mrs Arkhipov." Lucy blew on her pierogi before taking another bite.

"Do you think anyone will know what our costumes are?" asked Tex. He stroked his glued-on goatee.

"Not a chance," Lucy laughed.

"At least we have each other," Tex winked.

They clinked pierogi.

Pop music was blasting as Tex and Lucy scoped out the snack situation in the Pelusos' kitchen. The majority of the partygoers were out talking, dancing or standing awkwardly by the bonfire in the backyard.

Tex and Lucy each grabbed a handful of candy from a bowl on the countertop.

A pair of girls approached, one dressed as a bee, one as a witch. Both costumes included short skirts, for some reason.

Jaime and Amy, the bathroom twins.

"Are you supposed to be a Klingon?" asked Jaime, the brunette bumblebee.

"She is a Bajoran," Tex corrected her. "*I* am a Klingon." He pounded his chest for emphasis.

"Those are aliens, right?" Amy flicked her long blonde hair over her witchy shoulder.

"Obviously," said Jaime. "It's Lucy and Tex. That's, like, all they think about."

Jaimie's dad worked at the Nu Co. factory, where Lucy's father had recently been promoted to manager.

"Are there any eighth-graders here?" Lucy asked, casually unwrapping a piece of taffy.

"Why?" said Jaimie. "Looking for *Milo Fisher*?"

"Of course she is," Amy jeered. "She's, like,

obsessed with him."

"I'm not obsessed," Lucy scowled.

Jaimie whispered something in Amy's ear, and the duo giggled.

"Never mind." Lucy grabbed Tex, who was picking the green M&Ms out of the candy bowl, and directed him out of the kitchen. "When I find Milo, I'll let him know you think he's the hottest guy in school," she called over her shoulder.

"What!?" Amy's face turned bright red. "No!"

Lucy smirked triumphantly.

"Fish is the hottest guy?" Tex popped his fake teeth back in his mouth. "What am I, chopped liver?"

"You are what you eat," said Lucy.

Tex froze when they reached the living room. "Oh. My. Sandwiches."

"What?" asked Lucy, looking for Milo.

"That schnoodle Joey got the new Nintendo." Tex looked like he'd just stumbled upon the holy grail of happiness.

Resignedly, Lucy patted him on the arm. "It was nice knowing you."

Tex lumbered across the Persian rug, zombie-like, towards the flat-screen TV.

Feeling vaguely abandoned, Lucy stepped through the sliding-glass door into a cloud of burning wood, roasting wieners and pre-teen desperation.

Sticky Pines Elementary and Middle School (SPEAMS) had students all the way from kindergarten up to the ninth grade. There were at least three different class years present at Joey's party, all of them Upper. *Quite a coup for a seventh-grader.*

Lucy realised with a start that her and Tex's costumes were far more elaborate than anyone else's. *At least mine entails a leather jacket.*

Milo was by the bonfire, wearing a royal-blue suit and tie that brought out the colour of his eyes. On his lapel a patriotic badge read "It's morning in America!" He was laughing with a couple of eighth-grade soccer players in prison stripes that Lucy knew by reputation only.

She steeled her nerve and strode over. Milo's smile faltered.

"Hey, Fish," she said.

"Lucy," he responded coolly.

A girl in a Zorro mask ran over, yelled, "Assassin!" and threw a water balloon at the tallest athlete's back, drenching everyone in the vicinity.

"No fair!" yelled the victim. Laughing, both athletes chased after her.

"That game just gets funnier every time they do it," said Milo, deadpan. He shook water from his sleeve.

Have you forgiven me yet? thought Lucy. "What are you supposed to be?" she said instead. "A politician?"

"Clearly."

"Which one?"

"Do you know any politicians other than the current president?"

"No," Lucy admitted.

"I didn't think so."

Lucy fidgeted with her dangly earring. "What's, uh..." *I need to tell you the Truth.* "What's that red mark on your cheek?" *There are shapeshifters in Sticky Pines. Your dad wants to find them all and dissect them!* "Is it part of your costume or did someone egg your face?" *That didn't come out right.*

Milo glared at her. "Excuse me. I have to go to the restroom." He marched off towards the house, bumping past a mulleted theatre kid strumming a mandolin.

Deflated, Lucy slumped on to a log by the fire next to a girl roasting a marshmallow.

"Brutal," said the girl. She had short black hair with a fringe cut straight across her eyebrows, and a silver ring in her nose. A set of vampire fangs appeared to be the extent of her Halloween costume. Lucy guessed she was in the ninth grade.

"You're Mrs Sladan's kid, aren't you?" said the girl. "The one who found the missing people? I mean, not that they were really missing. They were being treated at the Nu Co. lab, right? Volunteer guinea pigs or something."

That had been the story on the news, at least.

The vampire slowly rotated her marshmallow. "You know, I've always found the 'official' explanation pretty far-fetched, myself," she said.

Say what now? The tips of Lucy's ears tingled. "Sorry," she said, "who are you?"

"Gertie Lee. Environmental activist and editor-in-chief of the *SPEAMS Sentinel.*" She held out a hand for Lucy to shake.

"You write for the school paper?" Lucy hardly ever read it since it never reported on UFO sightings.

Gertie nodded. "Have you ever thought about writing for the *Sentinel*?" Her marshmallow caught fire and she lifted it off the coals. "I'll bet you have quite a few stories to tell." She calmly blew out the flames.

Holy slug spit. Did this girl have extrasensory

perception? *Once again,* Lucy lamented, *I'm being offered a chance to expose the Truth, and I can't accept. Not until I know more about the Pretenders, at least.*

"I'm not much of a writer," she forced herself to say. She stood up, ready to leave before she told the girl everything she knew.

Gertie caught her by the sleeve. "Something weird happened at the factory, didn't it? And I'm not talking about gremlins or zombies or whatever you're into these days."

"How do you—"

"You have a reputation," said Gertie with a look of pity.

If the people at this school knew what was up, my reputation would be TRUTH CRUSADER, but okay. "What are you getting at?"

"They say weird things are happening at Nu Co." Gertie peeled off the charred outside layer of her marshmallow. "Half the students' parents work there, and they're all coming home late, acting tired and short-tempered. Your dad's a manager there, right?"

"Yeah." Lucy's dad *had* seemed grumpy lately… *Why?*

"Word on the mycelium network is –" Gertie looked around furtively – "Mr Fisher plans to profit by turning this whole town inside out. He's going to destroy the land, exploit the resources, then split when the sap's dried up." She popped the blackened marshmallow skin into her mouth.

"Really?" Lucy had been so concerned about the Pretenders she hadn't considered what Nu Co. was doing to Sticky Pines itself. A gust of wind blew smoke into Lucy's face, sending her coughing.

"Word is –" Gertie lowered her voice even further – "Fisher's working on something *freaky* over there."

"Like what?"

Gertie sniffed. "I'd have thought if anybody had inside knowledge, it'd be you." She held the marshmallow's naked interior over the flames.

"We could use a curious mind like yours at the *Sentinel*, Sladan. If you could stick to earthly matters, I think you'd make a great reporter. Nothing about mermaids or Sasquatches, though. The *Sentinel* is a serious paper."

Lucy shrugged. "Well. If you don't want me to write about anything interesting, what's the point?" She headed for the house.

"Suit yourself," Gertie called after her.

Back in the living room, Tex was surrounded by a group of kids cheering wildly. He was facing off against Joey in an epic fighting game showdown. Sweat beaded on his fuzzy upper lip as his pigtailed schoolgirl avatar did a running kick that sent Joey's mech-suited warrior flying helplessly into the void. The crowd roared as the schoolgirl struck a victory pose. Tex took a bow, then spotted Lucy.

Handing his controller to the nearest eager hand, he pushed his way through the throng to join her in the kitchen.

"Fish wouldn't talk to me," she told him, "but

I did score a job offer." She tore into a strip of taffy.

"I figured," Tex sighed. "He left the party a minute ago."

"He left? Because of me?" *Talk about an overreaction.* "His house is pretty far from here. Maybe we should go after him."

Tex patted Lucy's arm. "Leave the boy alone, Lucille. This is Sticky Pines. He will be perfectly safe."

"Right..." said Lucy. *I suppose that plague of monsters has been alleviated.* She glanced nervously at the front door. *What could possibly go wrong?*

CHAPTER 3

Making a Splash

Milo marched briskly away from Joey's Halloween party. He wasn't ready to talk to Lucy, not yet, and he certainly wasn't going to tell her all about his terrible day. She clearly couldn't stop herself from prying into his affairs. *She's like a yacht salesman. She never lets up.* In truth, it was one of her best qualities – but it was infuriating.

The setting sun cast long shadows through the trees. The neighbourhood was filled with the sound of laughing children and the scent of burning leaves. A woman dressed as a rag doll chased a brood of costumed kids swinging candy-filled buckets shaped like jack-o'-lanterns. One was a superhero, another a princess. Another wore a hairy, wolfish mask.

Milo felt a chill, remembering the beasts he and Lucy had encountered the previous month. He pulled his cashmere overcoat close. *Maybe I should call for a ride home...*

His stepmother had dropped him off less than an hour ago. Hopefully she was still free to come pick him up. *If she hasn't gone to a book club, or a wine tasting, or a Mercedes-only drag race.*

Milo pulled out his latest smartphone, which was protected by a shatter and waterproof case. *No reception, yet again. This town's infrastructure is seriously subpar.* The only mobile Milo had seen get reliable reception in the Big Crater Valley was his father's military-grade device. *Seems I'll be walking home. Oh joy.*

The road curved, turning into a bridge over the rapidly flowing Ungula river. To get home, Milo calculated, he would need to follow the river north, then travel halfway round the enormous lake for at least a couple of hours. Through the woods. In the dark. Milo swallowed. *At least my phone has a flashlight.*

The night darkened as he turned off the road on to a woodland path. High up in the trees, a night bird screeched, sending Milo's heart booming. *It's probably just a stupid owl...* He was regaining his composure when he heard a dull, mechanical buzzing sound, too quiet to be a helicopter, too loud to be a bumblebee. Looking up, he spotted four blue lights glowing faintly by the treetops.

He breathed a sigh of relief. *It's just one of Nu Co.'s drones. Wait... Is Dad keeping tabs on me after what happened this morning?* Milo reckoned he'd have to inspect the soles of his shoes later for a tracking device. *At least he cares, I guess.*

The surveillance drone drifted down for a closer look when it was abruptly snatched out of the air by a large, stripy owl. Milo jumped in alarm.

The owl swooped behind an evergreen, the

drone in its talons, and disappeared into the forest.

Milo knew better than to feel shocked. The feathered inhabitants of Sticky Pines often behaved rather strangely. *Well. That bird's family is going to be disappointed come dinnertime.*

He hastened his pace homewards, soon reaching Black Hole Lake. It was properly night-time now. The moon hung low on the horizon, casting a silvery path along the steaming water.

Shallow waves lapped against the shore. Milo checked the time. *This walk is taking longer than I'd hoped.* At his current pace, it would be at least three hours before he was even close to home.

Flippin' fantastic. This day just keeps getting better. He picked up a fist-sized rock and chucked it into the water, where it landed with a satisfying KER-PLOP!

That felt good.

He picked up another rock and threw it even harder. KER-PLOP! And another. KER-PLOP! And one more. THONK!

Milo winced at the hollow wooden sound. He'd hit something. He ran to the edge of the embankment and shined his light downwards. Floating untethered near the lake's edge was a small rowboat. Milo suspected someone had forgotten to tie the boat up, and it had floated away from its mooring.

He considered his options. If he took the boat and cut across the lake, he could reduce his journey by half. *Looks like I'm going out on the lake today after all.*

Finding no path to the narrow beach, Milo scrambled down the crumbly slope, scuffing his freshly polished brogues.

The rocks below were covered with black algae that may as well have been crude oil, it was so slippery. Milo took off his shoes and socks and rolled up his trousers.

Struggling to stay balanced, he waded into the water and caught the side of the boat. He tossed his shoes inside and scrambled in after them.

Orienting his position with his phone's

compass, he took hold of the oars on either side and propelled himself due north.

Soon, Milo was rowing in a comfortable rhythm. The summer he'd spent training with Harvard's crew team really seemed to be paying off. *Dad was right about one thing: it pays to be well rounded.*

It was eerily quiet out on the lake, with no sound but the rush of water as Milo paddled. To cheer himself up, he started whistling the first song that came into his head, which happened to be the theme to the 1950s TV show *Lassie*. "PHEW-EEEE-OOO, WOO-EEE-EEE-WOO-WOO..."

He rowed faster, his whistles echoing across the glassy water, a song reaching out into the abyss. Milo was near the middle of the lake, quite far from shore, when he noticed that his feet didn't seem to be getting any drier. He stopped whistling and looked down. There was a puddle in the bottom of the boat up to his ankles. His stomach turned as he realised that the boat was slowly filling up with water. *Leaping Lehmans. There's a leak.*

Frantically, he tried to locate a hole, to no avail. *Of course this boat didn't come unmoored on its own. Of course somebody abandoned it on purpose. What was I thinking? Foolish, stupid, reckless…*

Milo took a deep breath. He was halfway across the lake. If he went quickly, he might still make it to the other side. He started to row when he heard someone whistle the first few notes of the *Lassie* song.

There were no other boats around. Was it coming from the shore? "Hello?" Milo called.

The whistle sounded again, "PHBEEWWW-BEEEEEEE-BWOOOO." There was a slight trill to it, as if someone were whistling and blowing bubbles at the same time. Was someone out swimming on this cold October night?

Unbelievable. This town really is filled with kooks and crazies.

KER-THONKSHP! Something heavy landed inside the boat, splashing puddle water on to

Milo's face.

"Gah!" He felt around the boat and pulled up a fist-sized rock. "Who threw this?" His voice echoed across the silent depths. There was no response. He looked up, half-expecting to see the drone-snatching owl taunting him from above, but he saw nothing but celestial objects in a sparsely clouded sky.

Something moved to the right of the boat, distorting the moon's reflection on the water. Milo swore he could hear the faint sound of laughter.

"Who's there?"

The boat rocked as something brushed against it from underneath. Something big. Panicked, Milo started rowing with all his might. He was startlingly aware that his craft was now dipping perilously low under the weight of the growing puddle. He was sinking.

Note to self. He panted, red-faced. *Never go out in Sticky Pines alone.* He was practically flying through the water now. *Never go out in Sticky*

Pines at night. He gasped as something pulled at his oar. *Never leave home in Sticky Pines, period!*

Forcefully, the paddle was yanked out of Milo's hand. He yelped as it slid out of its socket and slipped under the water with a sad little PLOOP. He was now stranded. Then, just a metre away, he saw something emerge from the gloomy depths.

The water rippled as something thin and dark rose above the surface. Milo's chest tightened. *Is that a snake?* If it was, it was the biggest one he'd ever seen. He vaguely remembered something Lucy had said about an abyssal sea serpent in Black Hole Lake. *Are ALL her nonsense beliefs actually real?*

With quavering hands, he held out his flashlight-phone like a protective talisman. Another serpent popped up to his left, followed by two more behind him, and one more at the front. Milo gulped. *I'm surrounded.*

Another serpent slithered quickly up the side of the hull. Milo squealed, picked up one of his shoes and threw it at the snake with a THOCK. The slimy creature slurped back into the murky deep.

Milo squinted at the water, where he could just make out a large shadowy form below the surface. *Those aren't serpents*, he realised. *They're tentacles!* He was floating directly above a giant squid-like creature, whose arms were encircling his boat like a hand about to snatch an apple from a tree.

The puddle was halfway up Milo's shins now, the boat barely staying afloat. He pulled the remaining oar out of its socket and wielded it as a weapon, jabbing at the closest tentacle. Lightning quick, it slithered up the paddle and slurped against Milo's hand with an unsettling cold fishiness. Milo shrieked, lost his balance, and fell into the lake.

The good news was that the water was not as cold as he'd expected. That's where the good news ended. Milo coughed and sputtered, choking each time his head dipped below the surface. He'd received swimming lessons from an ex-Navy Seal, but right now he couldn't even remember how to float. Keeping a tight hold on his phone, he shook off his heavy overcoat, which drifted downwards, its sleeves flailing like a drowning man.

Something slimy caressed Milo's bare foot. *This is it, I'm a goner. And I'm going to die dressed as a politician.* A wave of pitiful acceptance washed over him as he sank into the gloomy depths.

Straining to hold his breath, Milo opened his eyes and held out his illuminated smartphone. If he was going to be eaten alive, he wanted to see what would be digesting him. The torchlight filtered through the murk, providing a hazy glimpse of an immense creature unlike anything Milo had ever seen. At its rear were eight tentacles, each as long as the rowboat. Its front half was that of a hideous, primordial fish with jagged teeth the size of bowling pins. *What is that Thing?*

Above, Milo could hear the faint sound of a

motor. Was someone else up there?

The octopodal monster swam closer, watching Milo with plate-sized orange eyes, its pupils horizontal black slits.

Nearly out of breath, Milo let out a bubbly scream.

Lightning fast, the Thing splayed its arms out in every direction, like a dark star. Its skin changed colour, alternating black, ivory and purple splotches that swirled hypnotically.

Mesmerised, Milo watched as the colour suddenly drained from the creature's nose, down its torso and along its tentacles until its entire body was moon-white.

What in the ever-loving...

One by one, the Thing gathered its ivory tentacles at the top of its head and formed a two-pronged tree-like structure.

Are those ... antlers? Milo was reminded of the stag they'd hit with their car that morning. *Did this Thing eat the deer?*

The motor above grew louder until it was

almost deafening.

Is it going to eat me? Regaining his terror-stricken senses, Milo inhaled a mouthful of water as he struggled to swim to the surface, which seemed an eternity away.

Then he felt something soft and solid beneath his feet. Nudging him with its wide, flat nose, the Thing propelled him forcefully out into the night air with a SHPLOSHK!

Shuddering and coughing, Milo clung to the prow of his half-submerged boat, the buzz of the motor echoing around him. He searched desperately for the mysterious creature, but saw no sign of it.

A bright headlight shone in his eyes.

"Milo!" yelled his stepmother.

Silver-blonde ponytail flying, Kaitlyn sped her jet ski over to the sputtering boy. She slid to a stop, reached down and, with Pilates-honed strength, lifted her soggy stepson on to the back of the vehicle.

"What were you thinking?" she demanded.

"Going out on the lake at night, all alone." She was wearing a sparkly pink wetsuit. "Your father is going to FLIP HIS LID." She smoothed Milo's hair with her manicured hand. "When he called me, saying he'd lost your signal over the water..." She exhaled, hand on her chest.

My signal? So he really was tracking me... "I was j-just trying to get h-home," Milo stammered through chattering teeth.

"Are you hurt?"

"I'm all right." *I think.* "Did you s-see anything weird out here?"

"Weird? No." She squeezed the water out her hair. "Not until I found you here, flopping around like a dying seal. Why?"

"I—" Milo stopped. Should he tell her? How would he even begin? "Nothing. Forget it." Deep in thought, he wrapped his arms round her waist. "Let's go home."

Kaitlyn sped the jet ski towards the shore, leaving the ill-fated rowboat to sink into the depths, joining whatever else lurked below.

CHAPTER 4

Turtle Boy

"Are you done yet?" Willow whined. "I'm booooored." She lay upside down in her chair, her pigtails dangling on the threadbare blue carpet.

Lucy thumbed through a thick tome entitled, *Signs, Designs and Crooked Lines: An Illustrated Guide to Symbology*. Haphazard piles of books on linguistics and ancient mythology adorned the desk around her.

"Go read a picture book or something," said Lucy.

"I've read them alllllll."

They were waiting in the school library for

their mother to finish grading so she could drive them home. For Lucy it was an opportunity to investigate.

Her battered notebook lay on the table before her, open to a page covered in drawings of the mysterious hieroglyphs she'd seen on the stone steps beneath the Nu Co. factory. One looked like a leaf with an arrow through it. One was a series of triangles with dots around them. Another resembled a lollipop.

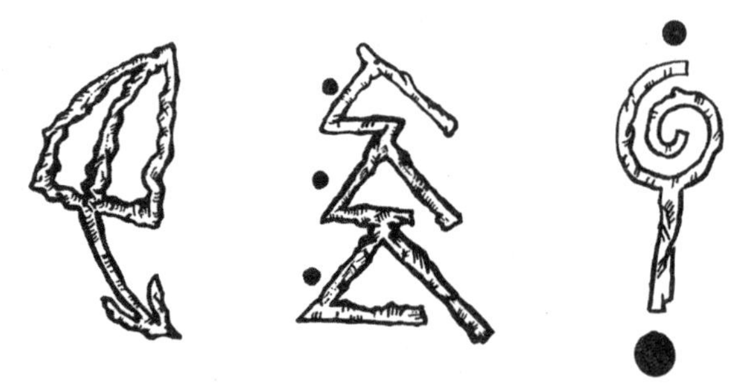

According to Mr Fisher's scientists, the glyphs meant: "Beware the Pretenders". Lucy knew exactly who the "Pretenders" were: the Strickses, Mandy Millepoids and the rest of Fisher's victims, because they were only *pretending* to be human.

But who'd made these glyphs? What language was it? Did the warning mean the Pretenders were dangerous? The origin of the symbols was one small mystery amongst many, but since nobody would talk to her, it was the only trail Lucy could follow for now.

Willow slid to the floor and pulled a musty hardback book off the nearest shelf.

"Ah, you found one of the old school yearbooks," said Ms Keisha. The young tattooed librarian pushed past Lucy and Willow with a cartful of books. "Pretty neat, huh?"

Lucy narrowed her eyes at the cheery woman. *Could she be one of Them?* She imagined Ms Keisha's tattoos squiggling around, her skin jellifying as she gooped into a bat or something and flew out the window.

Willow wiped the dust off the title: *SPEAMS Dreams*. "I wonder if Dad's in here." She opened the crumbling cover.

"If you find him, let me know immediately," said Lucy. "I'll bet his hair was INSANE."

Willow laughed so hard she snorted.

"Girls," said Ms Keisha, "this is a library, you need to keep it down." She tapped a poster on the wall from the 1900s featuring a cartoon kangaroo saying, "SSSHHH!"

"Yes, ma'am." Lucy saluted. She skimmed through her notebook to a page where she'd scribbled some of the questions and riddles rattling around in her brain: "Is it the trees?" "Does the sap make the Strickses turn into owls?" and "Note to self: eat a bunch of tree sap." The last sentence was crossed out, a vomit-faced emoji drawn underneath with the words "unsuccessful attempt" scrawled next to it.

"Oooh, look what I found," Willow whispered. She slammed the book on the desk and flopped it open. The pages were yellowed and worn, with drawings of big-eyed animals doodled in the margins.

Lucy examined the date in the corner. "1925? I'm pretty sure Dad's not *that* old."

"Not Dad. Look." Willow flipped to a page

with several black-and-white student portraits.

The people in the photos were all around Lucy's age, but their overly styled hair, formal clothing and steely expressions made them seem much older. Willow tapped a picture of a girl with chin-length pin-curled hair.

Lucy read the name under the picture and her eyes widened. *Esther Stricks.* "The Other Mrs Stricks?" She checked the date again. "It can't be. If she was twelve in 1925, that would make her, like, over a hundred years old." *Although she can turn into a bird, so what else might be true about her?*

Willow's lip curled in ambivalence. "I can never tell how old adults are."

Lucy thumbed through more student portraits and spotted another familiar name. "Alastair Chelon. Okay, I *know* he's not a hundred. He works with Dad, and they're basically the same age." She examined the skinny ten-year-old boy wearing a suit. *Is it really him? Can he turn into a bird, too?*

"Maybe it's his great-grandpa?" Willow suggested.

"That's a possibility," said Lucy. She crossed out the word "werewolves?" in her notebook and added "vampires?" under the word "ALIENS??"

She perused the rest of the portraits but didn't spot any other names she recognised. Near the back of the book, she came across group photos for various school clubs and activities.

Esther Stricks was pictured at the centre of the girls' basketball team, a head taller than everyone else. Lucy smirked at their attire, which looked like sailors' uniforms with pouffy skirts gathered in the middle to create makeshift shorts. *How can you dribble a ball in something like that?*

Next, she found a photograph of the "Arts and Crafts Society", in which little Alastair Chelon stood proudly next to his painting of a tortoise. *That's not bad, actually, for a ten-year-old.* She squinted at the picture, then gasped. The tortoise's intricately designed shell was covered in symbols like those she had seen under the Nu

Co. factory.

He's definitely *one of them.* "I'm on to you, turtle boy."

"What?" said Willow, perusing a yearbook from 1963.

"I didn't say anything." Lucy shook herself from her reverie. "You're hearing things again."

"Nice try, gaslighter." Willow stuck out her tongue.

Lucy raised her hand so high she was straining.

Ms Keisha looked up from the cartful of books she was shelving. "Yes, Lucy?"

"Can I please check out this book?" She held it up.

The librarian shook her head. "Those yearbooks are too old and fragile. They're for reference only."

"But this is an emergency," Lucy insisted.

Ms Keisha put her hand on her hip. "No, Lucita."

Pickled beets, this woman will not be moved.

Just then, Miranda Sladan strode into the

library, a canvas satchel overstuffed with papers slung round her shoulder. "All right, girlington bears, are you ready to go home?"

"Finally." Willow gathered her things.

Yeeps. "Just a minute," said Lucy. *What am I gonna do?*

"Got your grading done early today, Miranda?" said Ms Keisha.

Miranda patted her satchel and strolled over to the librarian's book cart. "Yes, hallelujah! I sense a big bar of dark chocolate in my near future. Sy and I are hoping to have a date night this evening, too, if Nu Co. doesn't have him working late again."

While they talked, Lucy bit her lip and prepared to do something positively *sacrilegious. It's all in service of the Truth*, she repeated to herself. As quietly as she could, she tore the turtle page out of the yearbook. Grimacing, she folded it up and slipped it into her pocket. She shut the yearbook, creating a small cloud of dust. "Okay," she croaked, "I'm ready."

"Great," said Miranda. She said goodbye to Ms Keisha and led Willow out the door.

I've got what I need, thought Lucy. *Alastair Chelon can fill in the rest.* She was formulating a plan to confront the suspected Pretender, but to pull it off she was going to need something harder to obtain than authentic alien autopsy results: her parents' permission.

CHAPTER 5

Woo Woo

What was *that Thing?* Milo had been ceaselessly replaying the events of Halloween in his head. *Was it some kind of mutant octopus? Was I hallucinating?* He thought of all the ways his assumptions had repeatedly been proven wrong since he'd arrived in Sticky Pines. *Is there really an honest-to-goodness monster in Black Hole Lake?*

He locked his silver bicycle to a lamp post across the street from The Woo Woo Store on the corner of Main Street and Ravenstone Way. It was the local "metaphysical" shop, specialising in incense, crystals and other nonsensical gewgaws. But, according to its out-of-date website, the shop also carried books on "supernatural phenomena" and, in particular, "local myths and legends".

The door chimes tinkled as Milo entered the store, the scent of sage overwhelming his senses.

"Welcome," said a serene female voice.

Milo stepped round a rotating display of dreamcatchers and spotted a rosy-cheeked woman with curly unnaturally red hair. She was threading a beaded necklace behind a glass counter filled with fairy figurines. Her blue-velvet dress wouldn't have looked out of place in the Renaissance.

Milo smirked at the crystal ball by the cash register. His late mother had had a deep appreciation for mystics, auras and the like, much to his father's chagrin. Milo wasn't really one to be taken in by any of this stuff. Still, he remembered that his mother had found it comforting when she was sick.

"Hi, I'm loo—" Milo tripped over a heavy

gnome statue.

"Are you here for a tarot or astrological reading?" asked the woman.

More like astro-illogical. "Uh, no, I was looking for something specific."

She smiled coyly, taking in Milo's khaki trousers and tucked-in sweater. "In the market for a love potion, perhaps?"

His cheeks reddened. "I'm looking for a book, actually. On legends from the Big Crater Valley."

She raised a hand to her temple, her bracelets tinkling, as if she were divining his thoughts from the ether. "I know just what you need."

Because I just told you?

The woman sashayed out from behind the counter and led him to a haphazardly organised bookshelf at the back of the shop. Running her ring-adorned fingers over the spines, she pulled out a well-read volume and handed it to Milo.

"*Sticky Secrets* by P. J. Barry," he read. "Is there anything about monsters in here?"

"Monsters?" she said, alarmed.

"My, uh, friend thinks she saw something weird in Black Hole Lake." Milo rolled his eyes to show that he, of course, would never consider such nonsense.

"I see." Lips pursed, the woman located a book titled *North American Cryptozoology.*

Lucy's obsession. Great. Milo deflated.

He followed her to the cash register and paid for the two books, which she put into a paper bag adorned with stars.

"Are you sure you wouldn't like a reading?" She gestured to a sign on the wall behind her: "Marietta Corbin, Fortune Teller. $10 for 10 minutes. CASH ONLY". "You look like you could use some insight."

"Oh, no," he laughed. "I mean, no offence, but none of this stuff is real, is it?"

"Everything is real," Ms Corbin replied, "though perhaps not in the way you think it is." She leaned in. "You know," she pressed, "some people do it just for fun."

Fun? Milo couldn't remember the last time

he'd had any. He glanced around. Nobody else was in the shop. "Yeah, okay," he acquiesced. "Why not?"

He followed her to a table covered in a black-lace cloth. Ms Corbin handed him a deck of cards, the backs of which featured strange glyphs made of shapes, swirls and dots.

"What do these symbols mean?" Milo asked while she shuffled.

"I made all these cards myself," Ms Corbin replied. "The symbols are just a Sticky Pines thing." She took the deck and dealt three cards face up on the table. "Intriguing," she mused.

The first card showed a picture of two rabbits standing on either side of a river. The second was a half-shaded moon with a smiling face. The third depicted a pyramid being demolished by a bolt of lightning, golden bricks tumbling down its sides.

Milo balked.

"That's not a bad card necessarily," Ms Corbin assured him.

Not necessarily?

She studied the spread, her fingers hovering over the images. Finally, she spoke. "You will soon learn that nothing is what it seems. Relationships, old and new, will be tested. What once was hidden will be revealed." She gripped Milo's hand. "You are in for a big shift in perspective, young man. Your world will be forever altered. Some degree of destruction is necessary." Her gaze intensified. "You must learn who to trust. Your choices will determine who you are to become. Change is coming, whether you're ready or not." Then she released him.

Milo picked up the pyramid card and examined it, horrified. *I thought this was supposed to be fun?*

"That will be ten dollars," said Ms Corbin sweetly.

He handed her a ten-dollar bill and quickly gathered his things and headed for the door. "That was..." He tripped on the gnome statue again. "Thanks."

"It was nice to meet you, Milo Fisher," she called after him.

"Yeah, you too," he replied, even though it hadn't been.

He opened the front door and ran smack into a not-so-little old lady.

"The Other Mrs Stricks," he gasped.

The older woman towered over him, her wild grey hair sticking out from under her beret. She and her wife (the school English teacher) had been among those who had disappeared during that unfortunate Nucralose-related business.

"Watch your way, boy." The Other Mrs Stricks straightened her pink woolly shawl. "You never know what's round the bend, do you?"

"Yes, ma'am," said Milo. "I mean, no, ma'am. Sorry, ma'am." He stepped aside and let her enter the store, the door closing behind her with a jingle.

Milo looked down at his hand and realised he was still holding that awful pyramid card. *Well, I'm definitely not going back in there*. Pocketing the item, he raced to his bike, jiggled the lock open, then hopped on and headed home. It wasn't until he was halfway down Main Street that he realised something that made him stop pedalling: he'd never introduced himself to Marietta Corbin.

So how did she know my name?

CHAPTER 6

Ghosts in the Machines

"What do you know about Alastair Chelon?" asked Lucy. She sat cross-legged on the wool rug in the wood-panelled living room of the Sladan household.

Miranda had driven Willow into town to buy a new pair of hiking boots, as her current hand-me-downs were falling apart.

"You mean the guy from the factory?" asked Lucy's father, tuning his banjo in the rocking chair. The only time he was able to play music these days was on the weekends. On Saturday mornings you couldn't prise an instrument out of his hands.

Lucy nodded.

"He's a quiet guy, keeps to himself," said Silas.

"How old is he?"

Silas noticed that Lucy had an open notebook on the coffee table before her, pen poised. His black moustache twitched. "Why are you asking questions about Al, squiddo?"

"I'm doing an article. For the school newspaper." Lucy said it just as she had rehearsed.

"You joined the *SPEAMS Sentinel*?" Silas rocked forward in his chair. "That's great! Your mom's been trying to get you to join for years. Did you tell her?"

"Not yet." Lucy forced a smile. This was a more enthusiastic reaction than she'd anticipated. *Great. I may actually have to join the paper. At least that'd be one less lie to keep track of.*

Silas plucked the first few notes of "Enter Sandman". "What are you writing about?"

"Nu Co.," said Lucy.

Silas stopped playing. "It better not be about

what happened at the factory last month," he snapped. "Nu Co. is going through enough trouble without dredging up that disaster."

"It's not about that," Lucy fibbed. "Why are you yelling?"

"I'm not yelling." Silas closed his eyes and rubbed his brow with a knuckle. "Sorry, sweetheart. I'm tired, that's all. What's your article about?"

Lucy chewed the end of her pen, going over the story she'd concocted in her head one last time. "Well, see," she said, "the *Sentinel* is doing a special on the history of the Big Crater Valley. I'm supposed to interview someone who works for the oldest business in Sticky Pines."

"Why don't you interview me?" asked Silas.

Good question... "It can't be someone I know," said Lucy, "because of 'Journalistic Integrity'." She dipped her head solemnly.

"Okay then," said Silas. "I'll give Al a call."

He continued tuning the strings on his banjo: BING, BING, BING.

Lucy sat quietly, staring at him.

"You want me to do it right now?" Silas grumbled.

"This is a REALLY important assignment."

"Oh for cryin' in the thunder flippin' rain." Silas set the instrument on the floor and stomped over to the landline in the kitchen.

Yeesh. So grumpy. Lucy stuffed her knees into her sweatshirt as she waited for her father to return. After what seemed like an hour but was probably ten minutes, he got off the phone and re-entered the living room.

"We'll meet Al at Buck's Burger Barn tomorrow afternoon," Silas announced.

Lucy jumped up in jubilance. *This is it!* Alastair Chelon was going to answer all her questions and she'd solve the mysteries of the Pretenders once and for all: who they were, what they wanted, where they came from, how they could change shape... *Wait*.

"Did you say 'we'?"

"I'm going with you. Obviously." Silas

laughed at the indignant expression on Lucy's face. "What, did you think I was going to let you meet a grown man you barely know all by yourself?" He chortled heartily. "Kids," he said to himself, "how do they ever make it to adulthood?"

Lucy fumed while her dad rocked out on his banjo as loudly as he could.

DINGA-BING! DINGA-RINGA-RINGA! The pinball machine by the haystack clanged as Lucy and her father entered the barnyard-themed restaurant. The town's only burger joint was packed with the Sunday crowd of hungry Sticky Pineseans dressed in their finest flannel. Lucy hurried past a smudged glass case showcasing a fake cast of a Sasquatch foot. Alastair Chelon sat at a table by the front window, which was already decorated for Christmas, eating a slice of cherry pie.

"Thanks so much for meeting us, Al." Silas pulled out a chair.

Alastair stood to greet them, wiping his hands on his corduroy trousers. He was a slight man with a sparse ginger moustache and shaggy strawberry-blond hair. His faded flannel shirt had a mustard stain on the sleeve. "No problem," he said. "I was on the school paper myself, when I was a kid."

"What year was that?" asked Lucy, sitting across from him. She dumped the contents of her backpack on the table, including several pens in varying colours, her mom's old tape recorder and a pocket-sized notebook she'd "borrowed" from Willow since her other one was full. It had a unicorn on the cover. That couldn't be helped.

Silas sat wearily. "Lucita, maybe we should order first."

"Sure." Lucy adjusted her glasses and switched on the tape recorder. "I'll take a hot dog. With fries. I'll mix the ketchup and mayonnaise myself."

"This kid's a crack-up," laughed Chelon.

"Would you like some more coffee, Al?" asked Silas.

"Ooh, yes please," said Chelon.

Silas waved at a waitress in braided pigtails and a blue gingham apron.

"Howdy," said the young woman. "My name's Michelle. Today's special is the Bigfootlong with sauerkraut and spuds. What can I rustle you up?"

She must be new. The servers rarely gave the whole spiel as the special never changed.

While Silas ordered, Lucy perused her notes. Since her father was there, she couldn't just dive straight into direct questions about Chelon's (*totally supernatural*) origins. She'd have to get creative.

"Let's start with what *Sentinel* readers really wanna know," Lucy began the interview. "What's your favourite animal?"

"Ooh, that's a toughie," said Chelon.

The waitress poured some steaming coffee into his mug.

"I like *owls* myself," said Lucy. She leaned in knowingly.

"I thought you liked the duck-billed platypus," Silas interjected. "Because everybody thought it was a hoax. Right?"

Lucy's nostrils flared. "Owls are my favourite *North American* animal, Dad."

Chelon sipped his coffee. "My favourite's probably the turtle," he said. "Because wherever he goes, he's home."

Lucy took down copious notes.

"I like coyotes," Silas offered.

"That's great, Dad." Lucy focused on Mr Chelon. "How long have you worked at the factory?'

"On and off since I was fifteen," he said. "This pie –" he picked off a piece of golden crust, which looked crisp and crumbly and perfect – "is just the best on the planet, isn't it?"

How many planets have you visited?

"They let you work when you were underage?" Silas chimed in. "I had to wait till I was eighteen."

"I may have lied about my age." Chelon chuckled.

Silas and Alastair had lived and worked in the same small town for countless years, Lucy realised, and yet her father didn't know much about him at all. *Why isn't Dad more curious about the people who live here? It's amazing how much information adults miss…*

"So, you have a habit of lying about your age?" she asked.

"Luce," Silas warned.

"How old *are* you?" she asked.

"You don't have to answer that, Al." Silas laughed, nervously.

Chelon smirked, a twinkle in his eye. "You wouldn't believe me if I told you."

Try me, Shifty.

The waitress slid Lucy's hot dog and Silas's melty cheeseburger on the table, then poured more coffee for the adults. Chelon added three packets of sugar to his cup.

That's a lot of sugar for a grown-up, isn't it?

"Where are you from?" she asked.

"Right here in Sticky Pines," Chelon smiled. "I've lived here since before I could crawl."

"And before that?"

"My people hail from all over the place." Chelon took another bite of pie. "Mmm-mm-mm."

Lucy swirled some ketchup and mayonnaise together with a fry. "What's it like to work for the oldest business in the Big Crater Valley?"

"Now, Al –" Silas held up a hand – "feel free to forget that I'm technically your boss now."

Chelon chuckled. "To tell you the truth, working at the sweetener factory was always a lot of fun."

"Was?" said Lucy.

"I still love the factory, it's just..." Chelon stared wistfully into his coffee. "I used to run the bottling machine, you see. I loved the splurty sound it made when you squeezed the syrup into the bottles. So satisfying."

Silas laughed. "Yeah, that was a fun job."

"What happened?" asked Lucy.

"Well, we're not bottling sweetener any more," said Chelon. "Not since the incident..." He cleared his throat. "Now we're just processing sap and putting it in barrels."

"And, boy howdy, is there more sap than ever," said Silas, wiping cheese sauce from his chin.

They were getting off-topic but Lucy's interest was piqued. "If you're not making Nucralose, why are you processing so much sap?"

"That's a good question. Do you know?" Chelon asked Silas.

"No idea," said Silas. "All I know is that they're expanding the orchard, and my orders are to make sure we increase sap production threefold." His face darkened. "When the equipment is working, that is."

"Ah yes." Chelon raised an eyebrow. "The ghosts in the machines."

Lucy's ears perked up. "Ghosts?"

"Not real ghosts," Silas cut in quickly, before

Lucy got the wrong idea. "Just … technical difficulties. The tree harvester keeps breaking down. The sap boiler won't boil, that kinda thing. You don't want to hear about it, Luce, believe me." He took a big bite of his burger.

Lucy recalled Gertie Lee saying something about people "fighting back" against Nu Co. *Could someone be sabotaging the machines on purpose?*

Lucy ate a couple of fries, then, as nonchalantly as she could, retrieved a piece of paper from her backpack. *Time to get down to serious beeswax.* Taking a deep breath, she unfolded it, revealing the page she had torn from the old yearbook at the library.

Chelon looked surprised, startled even. Lucy's heart did a somersault.

She pointed to the name next to the picture. "Do you recognise this boy?"

"I, uh," Chelon stammered. "Sure. That's my great-grandfather."

Sure it is, Alastair Chel-liar.

"Really?" Silas leaned in to look. "Cool!"

Lucy indicated the painting of the turtle. "Have you ever seen these symbols before?"

"Uh, maybe?" Chelon awkwardly sipped his coffee, spilling some on his shirt. "I remember seeing something like that in the tunnel under the factory. You know, where you found us that day."

Silas choked on his food. "Lucy," he coughed, "I told you not to bring that up."

Lucy pressed on. "What do they mean? Where do they come from?"

"I really couldn't say." Chelon's complexion paled.

"Okay, Lucita," said Silas. "You're done." He closed his daughter's notebook and shoved it in her backpack. "I'm so sorry about this, Al."

"Wait," Lucy begged. "I just wanna ask one last question." Then something passed by the window that caught her eye. "What is Fish doing with a big red kayak?"

"Is that some sort of riddle?" asked Chelon.

"Not fish," said Lucy, "Fish. As in Milo Fisher." She pointed.

Milo was walking past the burger joint, struggling to carry a shiny plastic boat more than twice his size. He was dressed in an assortment of kayaking gear, labels still attached, including water-resistant leggings, a nylon orange jacket and a front-facing backpack. Lucy figured he'd just bought everything at the sporting goods shop next door.

"Is he planning to take that thing to the lake on foot?" asked Silas.

"How odd," said Chelon.

"Yeah," said Lucy. "It is." She shot up, then wound through the tables and ran out the front door, knocking over a life-sized cardboard cut-out of a Bigfoot dressed in overalls and carrying a pitchfork.

As soon as he saw her, Milo dropped the heavy kayak on his water shoe-clad foot. "Ow!" he cried, hopping up and down in pain.

"Sorry," said Lucy. "What in the Crayola

crayons are you doing?"

"I'm optimising my stock portfolio," he said. "What does it look like I'm doing?"

Grunting, he lifted the boat to his shoulder and lumbered towards the bike rack, one end of the kayak dragging noisily on the concrete.

Lucy saw that he had tied a skateboard to the back of his mountain bike with a length of climbing rope. "Please tell me you're not gonna pull that boat down the road on that tiny thing."

Milo flushed. Clearly, that was precisely what he was planning to do. "Why do you care?"

Silas exited the restaurant carrying their uneaten food in a paper bag. "Hey, Milo. Good to see you." He handed Lucy her backpack.

"Hello, Mr Sladan." Milo tried to balance the boat on the skateboard, but it immediately fell off.

"Is your dad picking you up?" asked Silas.

"Nope," said Milo. "He said he'd take me to the lake yesterday, but he had to work. He's at Nu Co. again today, so I decided to show some initiative and go it alone." He sounded upset.

If Fish didn't hate me, I'd give him a hug. Or a handshake. Something.

"We'd be happy to give you a ride," Silas offered.

Lucy chewed her thumbnail. *There's no way Fish'll get in a car if* I'm *in it.*

Milo looked at his kayak, then over at his bike, then back at his kayak. He looked at his bike one more time. "Okay," he said to Lucy's surprise. "Thank you, Mr Sladan."

Silas grabbed one end of the boat and helped Milo hoist it off the ground. Lucy raced over to take the bike.

If Milo was willing to take a ride from Lucy and her father, he must be desperate. *What's so important over at Black Hole Lake?* She added this question to the list in her head of things she was determined to find out. A list that was growing longer by the day.

CHAPTER 7

Bait

They drove down the winding road in silence. Milo's kayak was tied to the roof of Silas's van, his bike and skateboard in the back. Lucy sat in the front seat, bouncing her knees. Milo could almost feel how badly she wanted to ask what he was up to.

Well, I'm certainly not going to tell her. He crossed his arms. *If you had any idea, Lucy Sladan, your brain would explode into confetti.* A sly smile crept on to his lips. *You're not the only one brave enough to investigate the paranormal.*

"So," said Silas, eyeing Milo's waterproof outfit in the rear-view mirror. "This your first time going out on Black Hole Lake?"

"No, sir," Milo replied. "I went for a very pleasant boat ride on Halloween evening, actually."

Lucy turned to face him, her lips pressed together tightly.

Is she holding her breath to keep from saying something?

"Why have you suddenly decided to take up solo kayaking in November?" she asked, the words spilling out of her.

"Why do you want to know?" said Milo.

Lucy scowled. "Because it's WEIRD."

"You should talk," Milo retorted. "You're the queen of weird."

"Is that meant to be an insult?"

"It's meant to be a fact."

"Why don't we listen to some music?" said Silas, louder than necessary. He switched on the car radio and turned the volume up high. The song "Don't Fear The Reaper" blasted ominously for the rest of the short drive.

When they reached Black Hole Lake, Silas left Lucy in the car and helped Milo unload his gear. Together, they slid the kayak into the lake.

"Do you know how to handle this thing?" Silas asked as he handed Milo the double-sided paddle.

"Yes, sir," he said. "I've been on pretty much every kind of boat there is." He slapped the kayak. "I've even got a life jacket." He retrieved it from the boat and slipped it on. "Don't worry, Mr Sladan." His extremely straight teeth glinted in the hazy afternoon sun. "I know what I'm doing."

Silas surveyed the calm water. "Your father knows you're here, then?"

"Of course." This was not true. In fact, Milo had wiped his phone and left his regular shoes in the dressing room at the sporting goods store to make sure he wasn't being tracked.

Silas scratched his neck. "All right, then. Be safe out there." He got back into the van and started up the engine.

Through the window Lucy kept her eyes on Milo as they disappeared round the bend.

Once the vehicle was out of sight, Milo locked his bike to a tree and stashed his skateboard in a bush.

Milo had eagerly devoured the books he'd purchased at The Woo Woo Store. The section on Black Hole Lake in *Sticky Secrets* had been especially interesting. It turned out that, over the years, there had been several unresolved and unsettling sightings of strange creatures, stretching back centuries to legends told amongst local Native American tribes. People had reported seeing a whole range of unlikely beasts, from large snakes to giant crocodiles and creatures resembling long-extinct dinosaurs. Occasionally, people had even disappeared while out swimming or fishing, never to be seen again. It had all been chalked up to unfortunate accidents, but rumours about the lake persisted, its murky waters and unfathomable depths still largely unexplored.

What was down there? Milo felt compelled to know. Whatever he'd encountered had had the chance to attack or eat him, but it had chosen not to. Why? And something else intrigued him about the creature… He could've sworn it was trying to communicate with him. Was that just his imagination? In any case, Milo was beginning to understand Lucy, his father and their respective obsessions better than ever before. Not that he'd ever tell them that. He pulled on his freshly bought fisherman's beanie and hopped into the kayak.

Aside from a man out fishing from a small boat on the other side of the lake, Milo was alone. The sky was a featureless backdrop of luminescent grey. A flock of geese flew by in a loose V, headed somewhere warmer. Milo snapped a quick picture of the birds with his new compact advanced camera, bought especially for taking artistic shots of wildlife.

After a half hour of paddling, he reached the area where he'd first seen the Thing. Rotating his aching shoulders, he whistled the first three notes of the *Lassie* song: "PHEW-EEEE-OOO."

He listened for a response. The wind rippled faintly across the surface of the lake, water lapping at the sides of his boat. Milo banged the kayak with his paddle, sending a low THOD-THOD-THOD out into the abyss. "PHEW-EEEEEE-OOOOO," he whistled again.

There was a splash behind him. Milo turned and saw a ring of ripples two yards away. *Something was just there.* He swore he could hear the faint trill of laughter. The hairs stirred on the back of his neck.

He banged on the boat and whistled again, squinting through his camera at the water's surface. Was something moving down there?

His thoughts were interrupted by the gruff puttering sound of an old motorboat approaching. It was the fisherman from across the lake.

Oh, come on. This guy's going to scare it off!

"H'lo, friend!" The fisherman waved.

Go away, stranger. Milo wearily waved back.

The man pulled his speedboat to a stop a few yards away. He was tall and portly, with a sparse goatee and a messy grey ponytail dangling from under a green cap. He looked familiar, but Milo couldn't quite place him. Of course, Sticky Pines was a small town. Lots of people looked familiar.

The man took in Milo's box-fresh kayaking getup. "You're not from around here, are you?"

Milo stiffened. *What's that supposed to mean? I bought a wool beanie and everything.*

"Oh!" The man slapped his forehead. "I know you. You're Lucy Goosie's buddy. Milo Fisher, right?"

The identity of the man dawned on Milo at last; he was the drummer in Silas Sladan's admittedly entertaining band The Sticky Six. Milo had seen them play at his father's carnival.

"And you're Steve, if I'm not mistaken?" Milo was fairly certain Lucy had introduced him as "Scruffy Steve", in fact. *It fits.*

Steve bobbed his head. "Say –" he glanced around – "you're not headed out to the Siren's Lair, are you?"

The Siren's Lair. Funnily enough, Milo knew exactly what Steve was talking about. According to *Sticky Secrets,* it was what the locals called the small island at the centre of the lake. Legend was that it contained a "spring of life" that could cure ailments and impart magical powers. However, the book assured the reader that this fanciful fable had been thoroughly debunked.

"I'm not going to the island," said Milo.

"Good, good. It's off limits to the public anyway," said Steve. "Protected habitat for bats, snakes and some kinda big spiders." He grimaced. "Yeah. Nobody goes to the Siren's Lair, that's for sure. I'm not one for rules, but I sure do follow that one."

"Cool, cool." Milo furtively scanned for any sign of the creature. *GO AWAY, STEVE!*

"Besides," Steve continued, "the island's really rocky, and, like, covered in brambles and super sticky pines. You know what happens when you get that sap on you, yeah? Hard to get off your clothes, man. Hard. To get. Off."

"Got it." *This guy sure likes to talk.* Milo held up his camera. "I'm just out here to shoot some pictures of birds and fish."

"Oh yeah?" said Steve. "Did you bring any bait?"

"Bait?"

"Bread? Frozen peas? Marshmallows?"

Marshmallows? "Uh ... no." Milo hadn't thought of that. Somehow he didn't think the monster would be interested in the kale salad he'd brought for lunch. He'd been hoping his whistling would lure it, like last time. Though, Milo pondered, perhaps his sinking boat was what had attracted the Thing. *Huh.* He gulped. *Maybe* I'm *the bait.*

Steve rifled through his cooler, then held up the biggest bucket of gummy worms Milo had ever seen. A large pink label on its side read "Mandy's Candies". "You can use these if you want."

"Wild animals like candy?" asked Milo.

"They do if it's from Mandy's," Steve replied.

Does this guy work there or something?

Steve tossed over the bucket, spiralling it like a football.

The container collided with Milo's hands as he threw them up to protect his face. The lid came off and neon-hued worms flew everywhere, raining into the lake in a series of PLOOPs. The bucket, still half filled with gummies, landed with a SPLOSH, bobbing as water slowly trickled in. Milo felt his ears redden with embarrassment. *All those extracurriculars, and nobody ever taught me how to catch a flipping football.*

"Whoopsie-daisy." Steve chortled, doubling over.

"I'd better get back to my photography," said Milo, praying Steve would take the hint.

Steve wiped a tear from his eye, then yanked on the rope-pull starter. His boat's motor garumphed noisily into life. "I'll see you 'round, Fisher." He waved as he sputtered off towards the shore.

Milo sighed. The candy worms floated pathetically around his boat, a fittingly colourful metaphor for the kaleidoscopic failure his day had become.

"PHEW-EEEE-OOO," Milo whistled. Nothing. No shadows. No splashes. No creepy laughter. Just the gloomy stillness of a cold November afternoon.

He took one last picture of the candy detritus, for artistic reasons, then morosely paddled towards home.

GLURGLESPLOOPH! A watery sound erupted from the lake behind him.

Milo turned round to look. Right where his kayak had just been, every single gummy worm had vanished, the bucket along with them. The surface on which they had floated was now frothy white, rings of disturbed water emanating out in all directions.

Something had sucked them into the lake in an instant. Something big enough to swallow them all in one gulp.

I knew something was down there!

With a SPHLUSH! the empty container emerged from somewhere far below. His heart leapfrogging, Milo paddled towards the floating bucket and retrieved it with his oar. He brought it close, then felt the blood drain from his face.

The clear plastic was marred with zigzagged scars of white from the marks of many, many sharp teeth.

The Thing. Milo's skin prickled. *It's here. And it's hungry.*

CHAPTER 8

Breaking Newsies

"I can't believe you joined a club," tittered Miranda Sladan, unable to hide her enthusiasm. "And it's not an extraterrestrial death cult; it's an official, school-sanctioned activity." She beamed. "The *SPEAMS Sentinel.*" She was actually beaming. "I'm so proud of you, *mija!*"

Lucy threw out a thumbs-up, as she packed her peanut butter and jelly sandwich into her planetary lunch box. Her mother's unbridled display of support was, quite frankly, insulting. *It's like the fact that Tex and I built a scale model of the Underground City of the Lizard People means nothing to her.*

Miranda rinsed her coffee mug in the kitchen sink. "Learning about *real* journalism instead of those crazy conspiracy theories will be a much-needed change for you, Lucita."

"What needs changing?" Willow entered the kitchen, dragging her glittery pink backpack on the floor.

"Your socks," said Lucy.

"My socks are clean," Willow protested. "They're from yesterday. Smell them."

"*You* smell them," said Lucy, pretending to gag.

"Smell them in the car." Miranda pushed her daughters into the garage. "What time should I pick you up after the club meeting?"

"I'll get a ride from the Arkhipovs," said Lucy, hopping into the van. "Tex is joining the paper too."

Miranda glanced at Lucy in the rear-view mirror. "Does *he* know that?"

"It was his idea." Lucy was really starting to wrap her head round all the lying it took to dig out the Truth. Besides, she was sure Tex would be thrilled to join the paper when she got around to telling him about it.

As she buckled her seat belt, Willow shoved both her feet under Lucy's nose.

"You want me to do WHAT?" said Tex.

He dug his heels into the linoleum as Lucy pushed him away from the cafeteria and towards the basement boiler room. The subterranean nerd-cave served as the newspaper club's headquarters. It was hot, windowless and smelled funny, but it was the only room with enough space for the club's printing equipment.

"We cannot join the newsies, Lucille," said Tex. "All they do is write about school elections and publish poems about recycling. Plus, they never eat."

The club was only supposed to meet twice a week after school, but the newsies were notoriously hardcore. Lucy understood the impulse to take a mission seriously, but these kids worked straight through lunch. Every. Single. Day.

"Lunch is sacred," said Tex. "It is a time of contemplation, rest and renewal."

"I know," Lucy agreed, "but I *need* this, buddy." She pulled him down a dank staircase that smelled like old cheese. "Maybe you can write video game reviews."

"You think games are all I care about, is that it?"

"They're not?"

"Goodbye." Tex turned round.

Lucy scurried past him and blocked the exit, bracing against cement walls that felt inexplicably greasy. "Please," she begged.

"I am more than just an alibi for your bonkers adventures, Lucille." Tex leaned against the wall. "Ew," he withdrew his hand. "Is that grease?"

"Maybe you can be the *Sentinel*'s new cartoonist?"

He looked intrigued, yet unconvinced.

"Plus," Lucy added, "the editor-in-chief has a nose ring."

"Gertie Lee is the editor of the school paper?" Tex ran his fingers through his unkempt blond hair, then grimaced as he realised his hand was still oily. "Well, I do like to draw."

"That's my guy." Lucy linked her arm with his and led him downstairs.

The dank room echoed with the tippity taps of *Sentinel* writers typing frantically at obsolete computers set up on folding tables. A dozen or so club members ran around, writing on whiteboards covered in log lines, tag lines and headlines: "The Price of Cafeteria Meatloaf Rises Three Cents", "What Your Spring Fling Attire Says About Your College Prospects" and "Is Principal Pakuna Selling Our Old Homework at the Farmer's Market? The Answer May Shock You!"

"If it isn't Lucy Sladan." Gertie hopped off a table in front of the rusty boiler. She was wearing a floral jumpsuit and combat boots. *Tex's soul is probably doing jumping jacks right now*. "Have you finally decided to put your story on the record?"

"Actually," said Lucy, "we're here to join the paper."

A small girl with wire-rimmed glasses ran past. "Just got a hot tip that the milk in the cafeteria is two days past its expiration date. Two days!"

"Go get 'em, Smitty!" said Gertie. She pointed from Lucy to Tex. "You two want to join the paper?"

Tex bowed. "You are looking at the *Sentinel*'s new political cartoonist," he announced.

"Political?" said Lucy.

"That is right, Lucille. I am fascinated by the inner workings of power in this school. The Machiavellian teachers and administrators who play with the student body like so many cats with mice."

Gertie took Tex in from head to toe. "I like your style. What's your name, kid?"

"Alexei Gregorovich Arkhipov at your service,

my lady." He bowed again.

Lucy wrinkled her nose.

"Can you really draw?" asked Gertie.

Tex proudly pulled out his binder and showed off the intricate doodles adorning the cover.

Gertie raised her chin approvingly. "We could use an artist with some actual skills. Not that everyone doesn't just love your 'ironic' stick figures, Dave," she called over her shoulder.

A curly-haired eighth-grader glanced up from his computer. "None taken," he said.

"What about you?" Gertie sized up Lucy. "Are you finally ready to dip your toes into the sea of reality?"

Tex snorted.

Lucy ignored him. "What you said at Joey's party got me thinking," she said to Gertie. "I'd like to try my hand at –" she leaned in conspiratorially – "investigative journalism."

Gertie tilted her head. "And what would you like to investigate?"

"I need a four-letter word for 'dishonest',"

shouted a boy from across the room.

"Wily," Gertie called back. "Bent. Base..." She searched for more synonyms.

"Nu Co.," said Lucy.

"Whoa." Gertie's eyes grew wide.

"Lucille," Tex warned, "you cannot keep sticking your nose into Fisher's business. Milo hates you enough as it is."

"Then this won't change anything, will it?" Lucy retorted.

Gertie contemplated Lucy's offer. "Let's talk somewhere more private." She ushered her behind a cluster of creaking pipes, out of earshot of the other newsies.

Tex sketched a bobble-headed portrait of Principal Pakuna on the nearest whiteboard.

"All right, Sladan," said Gertie, "you've got my attention. Shoot."

"Word on the mitochondrial network," said Lucy, "is that someone's been sabotaging Nu Co.'s equipment."

Gertie snapped her fingers. "So someone *is*

fighting back against the expansion! Maybe this planet isn't doomed by climate change yet."

"The planet is just as likely to be doomed by a giant alien laser cannon," said Lucy. "We are NOT prepared for first contact."

Gertie looked unamused.

"The point is," Lucy continued, "internal sabotage means that the workers have to put in extra hours. It's why they're all so miserable."

"Do you have any proof?"

"Proof's what I'm after."

"It's a front-page story." Gertie's eyes twinkled. "But –" she shook her head – "I can't let you do it."

"Why not? You were practically begging me to write for you."

"Yeah, about school stuff. The *Sentinel* isn't allowed to report on anything off-campus, ever since the incident with the hot dogs at Buck's Burger Barn..."

"That's bunk!" said Lucy. "This story IS school-related. Half the students' parents work there. Wait. What's wrong with the hot dogs at Buck's Burger Barn?"

"Sorry." Gertie shrugged. "If I'm going to be the first journalist elected president, I need this paper to run smoothly." She turned to leave.

"They're cutting down the entire forest between the factory and Black Hole Lake," said Lucy. "Did you know that?"

"That land is a habitat for endangered marmots." Gertie's eyes widened with fury.

"Fisher doesn't give two honks about marmots," said Lucy. "If you let me chase this up, I can expose him for the tree-munching monster he is."

"All right, Sladan. You've got your story." She held out a firm hand, which Lucy shook. Gertie cringed. "You touched the wall, didn't you?"

"One more thing," said Lucy, "I won't be at the club meetings after school."

Gertie frowned.

"I'll need that time to investigate, see?"

"Fine. Just don't get the paper into any trouble."

"Trouble?" Lucy slung her backpack over her shoulder and headed for the exit. "I don't know the meaning of the word."

"Then get a thesaurus," Gertie called after her.

"If we hurry –" Tex hustled up the stairs after Lucy – "we can still catch Hot Dog Monday."

"I'm not really in the mood for hot dogs," she replied.

They flung open the door to the main hall and almost tripped over a sullen eighth-grader sprawled out on the floor. It was Milo Fisher.

"Watch where you're going, Fishcake!" snarled an enormous seventh-grader towering menacingly over him.

"Are you okay, Fish?" Lucy knelt down.

"*He* bumped into *me*," said Milo, looking bewildered. He was holding the art room's bathroom pass: a full-sized toilet seat, spray-painted gold. The art teacher thought it was the height of humour.

"What the plop, Lars?" Tex puffed up his chest and faced the bully. "Milo Fisher is half your size."

"Everyone is half my size, pipsqueak," spat Lars. He sauntered off in the direction of the school gymnasium.

"Eat a snack, man," Tex yelled. "You are grumpy!"

Lucy helped Milo to his feet.

"What was that about?" he muttered.

Lucy furrowed her brow. "Well, Lars's mom works at Nu Co. . . ."

"What's that got to do with me?" said Milo.

"Uh, nothing." Lucy noted a pair of dark circles under his eyes. "Did you get any sleep last night?"

"Huh? How did you—" Milo faltered as somebody's overstuffed backpack collided with his shoulder. "I mean, well, there's this . . . Thing." He seemed to be having trouble finding his words.

It's like he really wants to tell me something but he's afraid to say it. "What is it?" said Lucy. "You look like a roadkill raccoon. What's going on with you?"

A group of soccer players led by that schnoodle Joey Peluso passed by, sniggering.

Milo stared at the floor. "I need to get back to class," he said. "Excuse me." He marched off down the hall.

Tex clucked his tongue. "Do you ever consider, Lucille, simply letting someone talk instead of interrogating them?"

"Something is really bothering him."

"And now we will never know what it is."

Lucy kicked the nearest locker. *So much for my investigative skills.* She led the way towards the cafeteria, visions of Milo's red kayak dancing through her head.

CHAPTER 9

The Reel Deal

Eyes half open, Milo paddled his kayak across the mist-shrouded lake through a predawn drizzle of rain. He'd arisen extra early this morning, and for once, he was completely alone. *Perfect.*

He'd been sleeping fitfully lately, plagued by dreams of endless dark waters with unseen monsters lurking below. Not helping was the sudden wave of cold shoulders and bullying he'd experienced at school; his fingers had been "accidentally" slammed in a locker, a group of kids simultaneously "finished eating" when he sat down to join them at lunch, and, of course, that Neanderthal Lars had pushed him down so hard his knees were still scabby. To top it all off Milo hadn't seen his father for five days in a row, which had to be some sort of record.

"PHEW-EEEE-OOO," he whistled, announcing his presence to whatever was out there. "Time to go fishing."

He unzipped his pack and pulled out a large bag of fat, juicy gummy worms from Mandy's Candies.

Over the past week, Milo had attempted to lure the creature with a variety of supermarket candy with no success. He eventually concluded that Steve must have been on to something, and that he'd have more success with Mandy's handmade confections. After all, everyone in town knew they were the best for miles around.

The day before, Milo had walked into Mandy's Candies wary of the fact that his father's alternative sweetener had previously turned the store's owner into a many-legged beast bent on destroying the Nu Co. factory. To Milo's relief, Mr Millepoids had greeted him with cool professionalism. Rather apologetically, Milo had bought some of everything the store had to offer, then, for good measure, tucked a twenty-dollar bill in the tip jar on the counter when he'd left.

The crinkling of the bag echoed across the lake as Milo emptied the candy into a netted pouch he'd secured to the end of a long rope. Closing the drawstring, he swung the bag over his head like a lasso, then released. The pouch flew through the air and landed with a PLURP.

Now, we wait. Milo took out his camera. His plan was to lure the creature close enough to capture a picture. *Come on, you preposterous beastie, get your breakfast.* There was a splash. Milo spun round so fast he felt whiplash in his neck.

QUACK.

An odd-looking duck with black-and-white plumage and bright orange eyes floated behind him. *False alarm.* The exotic bird swam over and pecked the side of his kayak.

"This candy isn't for you." Milo splashed the duck with his paddle until it ruffled its feathers and flew away.

Settling back into the boat, Milo's eyes glazed over as the dark clouds above turned orange, then pink. He yanked the rope a few times to make the pouch of gummy worms seem more enticing. Just as he was about to nod off, he felt a tug on the rope. Something was nibbling on the gummies.

Now wide awake, Milo wrapped the rope round his wrist and felt another nibble. It was working! But was it the lake monster or something else? The rope jerked again, harder this time, and Milo lurched forward. Whatever was pulling the pouch, it was big. Monster big. Abruptly, the line went slack and Milo flew backwards, his tailbone hitting the boat's hard plastic edge. "Ow." He rubbed his rear.

Rattled, Milo fumbled for the power button on his camera.

"Gyah!" he cried as the creature yanked the rope again. This time Milo braced himself, keeping his balance so the kayak moved along with him. His biceps felt weak from so much paddling over the last few days.

Another tug, another lurch. The kayak skipped along the lake's surface before sliding to a stop. Milo scanned the water with his camera, holding it one-handed. *Where is this Thing?*

Ripping open another bag of gummies with his teeth, he tossed a handful into the water and waited. The boat began to rock. Milo swore he could make out the shape of the enormous beast skulking below. *Keep it together, Milo. It didn't eat you before… It most likely won't eat you now.*

He snapped a few pictures as the water began to churn. The floating worms spun in a vortex, sinking one by one. With a start, Milo realised that his boat was being sucked into the swirling current. *Oh crum!* Frantically, he paddled backwards.

By the time he reoriented the kayak and had his camera ready, there was nothing left of the candy but a foamy patch of bubbles. A tentacled shadow loomed menacingly below, closer than before. All at once Milo felt very aware that his supposedly sturdy plastic kayak was actually quite small and fragile.

Rethinking his plan, such as it was, he searched for the nearest piece of land. A gust of wind parted a cloud of mist, revealing a patch of trees about a hundred yards away.

The Siren's Lair.

Scruffy Steve had said the island was off limits to visitors, but this was an emergency.

Milo was reeling in the "fishing" line when he felt something latch on to it. *Uh-oh.*

The Thing took hold and took off. The rope slid through Milo's fist, burning the skin on his palm. Instinctively, he slapped his other hand on to the rope, dropping his camera, which disappeared into the lake in an instant. *No!* There was no time to react. The kayak zoomed across the water, towed by the phenomenal force below.

"Grah!" Milo yelped as he was pulled towards the rocky island, fast. *Too fast.* The line was submerged fifteen feet in front of the kayak's nose, ribbons of white streaming behind it on the dark water. The Siren's Lair loomed larger and larger.

Milo let go of the rope and ducked to protect himself from the inevitable collision with the island. The kayak hit the shallow shore with a BRONCHHHH and Milo was thrown out, somersaulting on to the stony beach.

Twenty yards behind him, the creature circled back round, then swam straight at the shore, propelled by a body so powerful the water swelled in its wake. Milo could see the tip of its hideous slimy nose, below which, he knew, sat rows and rows of saw-like, flesh-tearing teeth.

As the Thing reached the shoreline, the enormous creature leapt out of the water, its tentacles streaming behind it like the angry flames of a rocket. Milo covered his head and screamed. He was abruptly hit, not by the monster, but by a wall of snot-like slime.

Trembling, he wiped the gunk from his eyes. The creature had vanished into thin air. Following the sound of galloping hoof beats, Milo turned and caught a glimpse of a stag, white as a ghost, disappearing into the dense island foliage behind him.

Milo lowered himself to the ground, his gooey arms wrapped round his shins. "That was… I just saw… Huh?" He tried to work out what had just happened. *That was the deer we hit. The one that ran into the lake. The monster didn't eat the deer, it…* His heart leapt in his chest. *The monster. The deer.* He gasped, choking on slime. *The deer IS the monster.*

"The Thing can change its shape!" he shouted to no one.

A surge of adrenaline flowed through Milo's veins. Flicking off the slime, he pulled his kayak up on to the island and dropped it on the gravel.

Breathlessly, he ran into the thicket where the unfathomable creature had vanished, venturing headlong into the unknown.

CHAPTER 10

Pink Smoke

Lucy informed her parents she'd be spending Friday evening researching a story for the school paper. They were still so thrilled she'd joined the *Sentinel*, they agreed to push her usual curfew back from eight to nine, no questions asked. *Pew pew!* While every word she'd told them was true, she had carefully avoided mentioning that instead of working in the boiler room with the other newsies, she would, *of flippin' course*, be heading to the Nu Co. factory, after-hours and alone.

Her plan was detailed, flawless even, if she did say so herself, which she did, to Tex, enough times that he threatened to block her on social media.

As soon as the last school bell rang at the end of the week, Lucy raced outside, hopped on her bike and pedalled like a hamster shredding it up on a wheel. The factory was all the way on the other side of the valley, so she'd have to hurry if she wanted to get there before dark.

In order to avoid being seen by any nosy parents, Lucy travelled via the small woodland path that circled Black Hole Lake. As the sun disappeared behind a curtain of clouds, a flurry of leaves flew up in her face. *Rude*. Shivering, she slid to a stop and zipped up her parka.

A hooting bird call caught Lucy's attention: WHOO-U-U-WHOO! She spotted a pair of owls with broad striped wings soaring overhead.

No flippin' way. Lucy hadn't seen the Strickses in weeks. *Is it them, or are those just regular owls?* The birds, whoever or whatever they were, continued eastwards over the lake. Was it Lucy's imagination, or were they headed to the factory, too?

Down below, she spotted a long red object nearing the creepy island at the centre of the lake. *That's Fish's kayak. Why is that doofus going to the Siren's Lair?*

The island had a sinister reputation. Some people said it was haunted. Some swore it was a refuge for murderers and thieves. Needless to say, it was a popular destination for anyone on the wrong side of a dare.

Lucy checked her calculator watch. It was getting late, and her investigation into Nu Co. was more important for now. The boy and his boat would have to wait. She pulled a dry leaf out of her hair, crumbling it to dust.

The woodland trail ended at a chain-link fence on the edge of Nu Co.'s property, beyond which lay a diminishing forest bathed in artificial light. The sound of buzz saws and heavy machinery echoed throughout the landscape.

Lucy hid her bike behind a blackberry bush

and tucked her conspicuous hair into a black beanie she had borrowed from Willow. It had cat ears. That couldn't be helped. She scrambled twenty feet up a slender fir tree and hid amongst its branches. Taking out a pair of binoculars from her backpack, she surveyed the scene.

A wasteland of felled trees lay before her, stretching to the edge of Nu Co.'s rapidly expanding orchard of sticky pine trees. Beyond the orchard, the factory puffed brown smoke from its pyramidal brick smokestack. From her perch, Lucy watched the last of the workers' cars cruise up the long factory driveway and exit on to the main road. Silas's faded yellow pickup truck was among them.

Lucy trained her binoculars to an area just past the fence where several large machines rumbled beneath the first evening stars. A towering yellow vehicle resembling a giraffe wrapped a complex set of saw blades round a tree, slicing it off its stump in less than a second. The mechanical beast spun the severed tree sideways and, faster than Lucy could say "crudberry pie *à la mode*", stripped off its branches and chopped it into logs, stacking them neatly in a pile.

Cripes and beans. At this rate the entire forest would be cleared in a matter of days, if not hours.

Hoping to get a closer look at the operation, Lucy slid to the ground and hopped over the chain-link fence. Slinking amongst the shadows, she crouched behind a pile of wood. The giraffe machine motored down the slope and gripped another tree, sawed it down, then–

POP-PA-PA-CROWW!

There was a bright flash and a puff of black smoke as the giraffe's saw blades suffered a series of small explosions. An alarm sounded and the vehicle released the tree before it caught fire. The driver jumped out and threw his hard hat to the ground. Meanwhile, a group of workers gathered around, shouting curses.

Lucy felt goosebumps. *Sabotage.* She tiptoed closer to the mayhem. Sidestepping a freshly cut stump, she tripped and fell face first into a patch of prickly ferns.

"Hey, did you hear that?" shouted one of the workers.

"Is someone over there?"

The shouts of the mob grew louder as angry footsteps crunched towards Lucy. She curled up under the fern's fronds and tried to make herself as small as possible. *These goombas are out for blood!*

"No, not there, over here!" someone shouted. "Some cornpone's behind the stump grinder!"

Now the feet were stampeding in the opposite direction.

Phew. That was close. Lucy crawled behind an alder tree and peered through her binoculars.

The workers surrounded a rhinoceros-sized machine with tank treads. It too was spitting sparks. Abruptly, they dragged a man wearing a grey fedora hat and an overcoat out from behind the vehicle and into the light.

"It's the weatherman," gasped the machine operator.

Lucy's breath caught in her throat. It was none other than Carlos Felina, handsome Sticky Pines newscaster. *And secret Pretender.*

An SUV barrelled down the dirt road that cut through the orchard and into the clearing, the words "SECURITY" printed on its side in white letters. It slid to a stop and three serious-looking men stepped out.

Great. Fisher's goons. The first time Lucy had seen these bozos, they'd been disguised as creepy clowns at the Nu Co. Par-T in Da Pines carnival (*ugh*). Today, they wore black suits and ties topped off with sunglasses, despite the low light. *They look like they're auditioning for* Men in Black: The Musical.

The hard-hatted workers thrust Carlos Felina towards the slickly dressed newcomers.

The weatherman raised his hands in surrender. "Please, I can explain," he began.

"Save it, pretty boy," snarled a thick-set, soft-chinned goon. It was Murl, Fisher's head of security. *And dillweed extraordinaire.*

"You're coming with us," said a tall, thin man at his side. Lucy had previously nicknamed this one "Tweedle Dum".

"Who else is working with you?" yipped the shortest man in black. *And there's "Tweedle Dummer", his partner in donked-up doofery.*

The weatherman cowered. "I'm… I'm…" He seemed to make eye contact with Lucy from afar.

Can he see me?

"I'm alone. I swear it."

Murl whistled and the Dums bundled Felina into the back of the SUV, then drove off into the orchard.

Where are they taking him?

Lucy snuck round the grumbling workers and hurried after the car. Staying out of sight, she ran through the rows of cultivated trees, each tapped and flowing with sticky black sap. *So much sap. But if they're not selling Nucralose, what's it for?*

The SUV's rear lights glowed red as it pulled to a stop in the middle of the orchard next to a curiously dense patch of trees.

Murl emerged from the driver's seat and Dum and Dummer pulled Felina out of the rear. They escorted the weatherman through a narrow pathway leading into the grove.

As soon as they disappeared, Lucy hustled across the road and crawled through the grove's underbrush. When she reached the edge of a clearing, she hid behind a low branch and peeked through the pine needles.

The dense trees encircled a white windowless geodesic dome about as wide as a school bus. A pipe stuck out of its top, emitting copious plumes of bubblegum pink smoke. A tangy, metallic scent hung in the air. *What in the Princess Peach is this place?*

In the clearing, Murl and his goons marched Carlos to the front of the futuristic building.

"This is all just a misunderstanding," said the weatherman tremulously. "If you'll allow me to speak to Mr Fisher, I'm sure I can clear this all up." He smiled like he did when he was on TV. "You see, I'm somewhat of a celebrity around here."

"We know exactly who you are" said Dummer. He and Dum led Carlos up a few steps to the dome's front door.

Lucy squinted through her binoculars as Murl typed a code into a number pad. *1-9-1-3-6-9.* She jotted down the numbers in her notebook. With a beep the door unlocked.

"Where are you taking me?" asked Carlos.

"Down," Murl sneered.

Dum and Dummer each grabbed an arm and pulled Carlos towards the entrance. This time he resisted, thrashing against their grasp.

Lucy fought the urge to cry out. *I need to help him! But what can I do?*

"Get in there," grunted Dum.

"No!" Carlos yowled like a wild animal.

Lucy jumped as she heard a gloppy SPLOOSH!

Dummer stumbled, his head clunking into Dum's chest as their arms closed round liquid slime. Carlos Felina had seemingly vanished.

But Lucy knew better.

"What the—" Dummer squealed.

"Where'd he go?" Dum stared in bewilderment at his goopy hands.

Standing at their feet was a black-and-white cat, its back arching as it hissed and spat with fury.

I knew it! Lucy was so excited she nearly dropped her binoculars. This was the first concrete piece of Pretender proof she'd witnessed since the Strickses transformed into owls. *Carlos Felina can change into an animal, too! What the slug ARE these people??*

"It's him, you idiots!" thundered Murl.

Cat Carlos screeched and high-tailed it into the trees, leaving Dum and Dummer slack-jawed.

"Go after it," Murl ordered.

Slipping on slime, Dum and Dummer chased the tuxedo tom, crunching through the grove pathway, just two yards away from Lucy's hiding spot. Murl shook his head with disgust, then entered the dome and shut the door behind him with a CLANG.

Lucy stashed her binoculars in her backpack and wrote furiously in her notebook about the events she'd just witnessed. Questions whirled in her head. What was in the dome? What was Nu Co. doing in there? Why did they need so much sap? And what was producing the pink smoke?

Only one way to find out.

She considered using the door code to sneak inside, but with Murl around it seemed too risky. Perhaps she could find some clues in the factory? Tossing her pack round her shoulders, and neglecting to check if the coast was clear, she hurried out on to the dirt road, straight into the bright beams of a car's headlights.

A silver sedan screeched to a stop, inches away from Lucy's quaking kneecaps.

"Watch where you're going!" shouted a razor-sharp voice. "Does everything in this town have a death wish?" A tall, broad-shouldered man exited the vehicle, looking extraordinarily cross.

Aw, crud.

"Lucy Sladan." Mr Fisher slammed the door to his car. "Once again, I find you trespassing on my property." Anger flashed across his face. "You wouldn't be here to *sabotage* company equipment by any chance?"

Lucy's mouth felt dry. Fumblingly, she fished something out of her back pocket and held it out. It was a small card, on which she had written "PRESS PASS" in black Sharpie. "I'm with the school paper," she asserted. "I've got Journalistic Immunity."

"That's not a thing," Fisher replied. He grabbed Lucy's backpack and roughly prised it off her shoulders.

"Give that back!" she cried.

He sifted through the bag's contents, tossing aside a print-casting kit, a wooden letter opener and a homemade grappling hook. He unzipped the front pouch and retrieved the unicorn notebook.

"I need that!" Lucy glowered. *If he reads*

it, he'll see everything I've learned about the Pretenders. Everything!

Fisher tossed the empty bag at her feet, holding the notebook out of reach. "You'll get this back when I'm done with it."

This is just great. Lucy gathered up her belongings, feeling flames of anger rise at her temples. She was in big trouble this time. Would he call her parents? *Skunk-faced dingus.* She'd be grounded for a decade at least.

"Come with me." Fisher's tone left no room for argument. He pointed into the thicket. "This way."

He was taking her to the geodesic dome. Lucy's toes went cold. "What's in there?"

"Your father," said Fisher. "I'll take you to him."

He was lying. Lucy had watched Silas drive away almost an hour ago. *What's Fisher's game?* Still, she did want to know what was inside the dome. And she couldn't leave without her notebook. She looked around the empty, moonlit orchard. What choice did she have, anyway?

Resigned, she turned to follow the sharply dressed businessman. Just then, the back door of Fisher's car opened and a middle-aged slip of a woman stepped out on to the road. The newcomer was clad in a floral sweatshirt, shorts and Birkenstock sandals, in flagrant defiance of the season.

"Mrs Stricks!" Lucy exclaimed.

Before Fisher could protest, the diminutive English teacher snatched the notebook out of his startled hands, then positioned herself protectively in front of her student. "That devil on your shoulder giving you ideas again, Richard?"

"How did you get in my car?" demanded Fisher.

There was more than a little mischief in Mrs Stricks's smile.

"I'm calling security." Mr Fisher took out his smartphone.

"How about this?" Mrs Stricks challenged

Fisher, who was at least a head taller. "You let us leave quietly, and we can all forget the fact that you just kidnapped a minor and tried to take her into that little laboratory of yours."

Laboratory? Was it possible that Fisher still thought Lucy was a Pretender? *What was he going to do to me?*

"What's with the pink smoke, Richard?" asked Mrs Stricks. "We both know you're not making candy down there."

Fisher narrowed his eyes. "Get off my property," he intoned.

"All you had to do was ask." Mrs Stricks winked.

Fuming, Fisher stormed off towards the dome.

Her short salt-and-pepper hair bouncing, Mrs Stricks hurried Lucy through the orchard to the long driveway. Surveillance drones hovered menacingly overhead as they made their way up towards the main road.

When they reached the far edge of Nu Co.'s property, they exited through the front gate.

Lucy's bike was propped up on its kickstand on the other side, waiting for her. *Whoa. How did it get all the way over here?*

She scanned the woodland surrounding the moonlit road. She figured that the Other Mrs Stricks must be lurking somewhere nearby, but she saw no one.

"You shouldn't have come here," warned Mrs Stricks. "Mr Fisher's got that 'gold fever' look in his eye. A man in that state can't be trusted."

"What are they making in that secret laboratory?" asked Lucy.

"Nothing you should concern yourself with."

"But I am concerned." Lucy gripped her bike's handlebar. "What could possibly produce pink smoke?"

Mrs Stricks gently patted Lucy's cat beanie. "Just focus on getting yourself home in one piece. Can you do that for me?"

"But—"

"Goodnight, Lucita." The teacher crouched down low, then flung her arms up and leapt into the air. In an instant her body quivered and liquefied as she transformed into a barred owl, splattering Lucy from head to toe with a surge of transparent slime.

The impish owl hooted what might've been an apology and disappeared over the forest canopy. Lucy scraped the goop off her glasses and shook it on to the asphalt.

Seriously, Mrs Stricks? Ew.

CHAPTER 11

Heart-to-Heart

Milo sat on a stool in the kitchen in his blue-striped pyjamas, waiting for his father to come home. He sipped from a mug of warm oat milk with a dash of turmeric and black pepper, then checked the clock again. It was well past midnight. He set the mug down. *Where is he?*

It had been two hours since Milo had returned home. Nobody had greeted him when he walked through the door, teeth chattering, still clad in his kayaking gear. There was a note on the fridge from Kaitlyn saying that she had an early spin class, and that dinner was in the fridge ready for reheating. Milo didn't feel hungry. He wasn't sleepy, either. He was nervous, because he was finally ready to tell his father about the incredible things he'd seen over the last week.

He drained his mug and slid it into the sink where it landed with a CLANK, the solitary sound reverberating off the high ceiling. He was just about to head up to bed when he heard the rumble of the garage door. A moment later, his father entered the kitchen, red-eyed, his tie loosened around his neck.

Spotting Milo, Mr Fisher straightened his shoulders. "You're up late," he said, making an effort to sound cheery. He tossed his suit jacket on a stool and set his high-tech briefcase on the marble floor.

"Dinner's in the fridge." Milo pointed to Kaitlyn's note. He fidgeted as his father rummaged through the refrigerator. "How was your day?"

Fisher set a bowl of steamed broccoli, Wagyu steak and quinoa on the counter and unwrapped the cellophane. "Long." He pulled up a stool at the kitchen island. His phone buzzed and he typed a response to a text.

Dad's not even going to ask me what I was doing today, is he? It had been like this for the past month, his father seeming more distracted, coming home later and later. The only thing they'd talked about in the last few weeks was how funny it was that birds kept mistaking Nu Co.'s drones for dinner. That, and Milo's dubious explanations for his perpetually missing shoes.

"Who are you talking to?" asked Milo.

Fisher put his smartphone away. "Sorry, pal," he said. "It's work stuff. You know how consuming it can be." He tapped his fingers on the counter. Milo hadn't seen him so agitated in a while. "I saw your little *friend* this evening." He gave Milo a pointed look, his fork poised over his food.

My friend? Milo nearly choked. *Did he track me down after all?*

"That girl broke in to the factory grounds. Again." Fisher took a bite of broccoli.

Milo realised who he was talking about. "Oh, you mean Lucy. She broke into Nu Co.?" *That's odd, but so is she.* "Why did she do that?"

"I was hoping you could fill me in."

"I have no idea what she's up to these days."

"I certainly hope not."

Okay, then. Moving on... Milo took a deep breath. He'd been preparing for this moment all evening. "Dad. There's something I need to discuss with you. Something very important."

Fisher exhaled, long and low. "I know," he said ruefully.

"You do?" Milo was fairly certain that he didn't.

"I'm still not making enough time for you." Fisher reached across the granite countertop and took Milo's hand. "The work we're doing at Nu Co. is so revolutionary it's hard to focus on anything else. But I want you to know that I think about you every single day."

He set his briefcase on the counter, checked the code on his high-security "watch", then input the number into the case's locking interface.

So that's what the code is for. Mr Fisher had been carrying that briefcase with him everywhere lately. Clearly, it contained something extraordinarily important.

Milo heard the rustling of papers as his father pulled something out of the briefcase then snapped it shut.

He handed over a picture of the two of them together from when Milo was a baby. Mr Fisher was dressed more casually than Milo had ever seen him, wearing a Hawaiian shirt with a tuft of chest hair showing. He held Milo in his arms on some tropical terrace surrounded by greenery, smiling as his pinky finger was munched upon by his fat-cheeked baby boy.

Mom must've taken this picture. Milo's mother had died of cancer when he was just six years old. She didn't often come up in conversation at the Fisher household, but Milo thought of her often. He wondered if his father did the same. Milo's throat momentarily felt too tight for him to speak.

"Son, I'm going to let you in on a little secret."

Milo's ears perked up.

"Sticky Pines has become more than a simple business venture. There are resources here you couldn't begin to imagine, and if I'm successful, Nu Co. will be the only company in the world with access to them." He caught Milo's gaze. "I'm building us an empire, kid, mark my words. And once all the kinks are worked out of the operation, which will be soon –" he said it as a solemn vow – "you and I will take a nice vacation. Someplace warm, where it never rains." He tapped Milo under the chin with his knuckle.

"Thanks, Dad," said Milo. It all sounded great, but he had more pressing things to discuss. "Speaking of Nu Co. . . ." He set down the family photo. "You know how, that day at the factory, your Nucralose formula caused some people to . . . to –" *Come on, just spit it out* – "transform into big hairy monsters? Basically?"

Mr Fisher froze, his fork laden with quinoa. "Allegedly," he said. "What about it?"

"Well," said Milo. "That proves that it's possible for a biological being to physically transform into something else, right?" He was pleased that he was sounding relatively coherent. "And if it can happen in one instance, it could happen in another. And maybe it could even happen *without* Nucralose." Milo noticed that his father had turned ashen. "Dad? Are you all right?"

"Have you been talking to the Sladan girl?"

"Huh? Lucy?" Milo scratched his head. *Why is he so obsessed with her?* "What do you mean?" *This conversation is not going the way I planned...*

"Stay away from her," Fisher demanded.

Milo was taken aback. His dad only used that tone when Milo was in trouble, which was rare, and he certainly hadn't done anything to deserve it now. *My dad seems physically incapable of listening to me tonight. I guess the Truth will have to wait.*

"Sure," said Milo, deflated. "No Lucy. No problem."

"Good." Fisher relaxed. His mind seemed to be very far away. "I have everything under control, don't you worry. Nu Co. is close to solving this Sticky Pines problem once and for all." He took a bite of steak and chewed.

Milo frowned. He had no idea what his father was talking about, but he didn't like the sound of it.

"Was there something else you wanted to discuss?" asked Fisher.

Milo feigned a yawn. "I think I'll head up to bed. It's been a long day." He gave his father a squeeze.

"'Night, kiddo," said Fisher, patting Milo's hand.

Heading into the hallway, Milo glanced back to see his dad staring wistfully at the old photograph before returning it to his briefcase.

Milo made his way across the spacious living room, nowhere nearer to feeling sleepy than he had been an hour ago, and ascended a wooden staircase that looked like it was floating in space.

CHAPTER 12

Serious Business

"Hello?" Lucy croaked into the cordless phone her sister had shoved in her face.

Willow yanked open the blinds and Lucy flinched as bright sunshine streamed into her small A-frame bedroom.

"Where's my article, Sladan?" Gertie Lee was on the other line, gratingly business-like for a Saturday morning.

Wh–huh? Lucy blearily read the time on the alarm clock, which she had not set. "It's eight a.m." she groused.

Willow jumped on to the bed and started bouncing around her big sister, her pink hooded poncho mushrooming around her.

Lucy waved her away. Bleary-eyed, she propped herself up on an elbow and retrieved her glasses from the nightstand.

"You don't come to club meetings and you don't have a mobile," said Gertie. "How am I supposed to yell at you for missing your deadline?"

Lucy caught her sister by the foot mid-bounce. The smaller Sladan landed on the mattress in a fit of giggles.

Somebody upped the sugar dosage at breakfast this morning. Lucy sniffed the air. *Cinnamon rolls. Hallelujah!*

"I'm still investigating." Lucy rummaged through her laundry basket and pulled out a pair of jeans. "This story is hot as pop tarts. I'm gonna need some time."

"You've had a whole week already," Gertie sniped.

"This ain't about spoiled milk in the cafeteria." Lucy tugged a green jumper over her head.

"There's some seriously mega shenanigans going on at Nu Co."

"What kind of shenanigans?"

Lucy tripped over Willow, who was crawling on the floor like a cat. "Knock it off, Will!" she barked. "Look, Gertie, when people read about what I saw last night, it will BLOW THEIR MINDS. We're talking secret labs. Sabotage. Pink smoke." *Shapeshifting*. "This piece is gonna be stratospheric, I guarantee it."

"Pink smoke?" said Gertie.

Lucy caught her reflection in the full-length mirror, grimaced and patted down her bedhead.

"I need this juice ASAP," Gertie insisted. "Nothing happens in November, outside of parent-teacher conferences and the inevitable controversy over Native American representation in the Thanksgiving pageant."

Lucy grabbed her backpack and jumped over Willow on her way out to the landing. "At least give me till Monday."

"Fine, but this better be front-page material,

Sladan," said Gertie. "I'm using this year's *Sentinel* for my Stanford application, and I need AT LEAST six years of extreme extracurriculars."

"You won't be disappointed, Gertie. This one's for the ages!" Lucy hung up without saying goodbye, like she'd seen reporters do in movies. She sidled into the kitchen, inhaling the sweet smell of cinnamon and butter.

Her mother looked up from her newspaper. "You're up early."

Silas checked the ceramic sun-shaped clock over the sink where he was doing dishes. "Whoa, it's not even ten yet."

Lucy grabbed a cinnamon roll from the baking tray, poured herself a pulpy glass of fresh orange juice and downed it in one gulp.

"Going somewhere?" Miranda eyed Lucy's backpack.

"I'm on assignment for the *Sentinel*." Lucy scarfed down her roll.

"How is the paper going?" asked Silas, drying

his hands. "Did your editor like our interview with Alastair?"

"I'm still writing it up, but I know everyone's gonna go mad for it," Lucy winked. She kissed her mother on the cheek, grabbed her hat and parka from the hook by the door, and hurried into the garage.

Right. Now to answer the eternal question: is this plan gonna work? Going over the checklist in her notebook, she rummaged through a stack of cardboard boxes and pulled out two deflated inner tubes and a bicycle pump. Next, she located a coiled length of rope in the cupboard above the washing machine. Lastly, she folded up an empty cardboard box, then stuffed it all into her backpack, which, try as she might, wouldn't zip all the way.

Lucy hopped on her bike and headed out to the road, keeping her fingers crossed for good luck. She was going to need it.

CHAPTER 13

The Thing

The cold nipped at Milo's toes as he crunched across the island shore in his water shoes. He'd arrived at the Siren's Lair bright and early in his quest to track down the Thing. Today it was proving more elusive than ever. Once more, Milo whistled, hoping for a response. "PHEW-EEEE-OOO." None came.

A few days before, Milo had managed to get within an arm's breadth of the creature by hiding in a fir tree at the far side of the island. He'd spent three uncomfortable hours waiting, reading *Sticky Secrets* to pass the time. *This town's history is truly insane.* At last, the white stag emerged through the foliage and nibbled on the sweets Milo had scattered on the ground below. Milo had moved to get a closer look, but he lost his footing and dropped the heavy book. Immediately, the deer spooked and bounded off. Milo slid down as quickly as he could and gave chase, but the creature had vanished faster than the spectre of fiscal responsibility at the Federal Reserve.

Now, after a couple days of careful tracking, Milo felt he had a handle on exactly where the Thing was hiding.

Ducking under a broken sign that read "Restricted Area: Trespassers Will—", Milo entered a sheltered clearing in a copse of leafless alders and indigo sticky pines. He set his pack behind a shoulder-high boulder covered in layers of graffiti, some of which was carved into the stone itself.

On the far side of the clearing, ringed by a sprinkling of white-capped mushrooms, was a bubbling hot spring no wider than Milo's waist. He'd be willing to bet his Burberry brogues that this was, in fact, the fabled "spring of life" mentioned in *Sticky Secrets*. At first glance it certainly didn't seem "mystical" or "magical", and its scalding waters smelled like boiled eggs. But, Milo reasoned, perhaps what made it "special" wasn't what it *did*, but what it *contained*.

He had realised the day before that this small stinky spring would make a perfect hiding place. Of course, the Thing was much too big to fit inside, but if it could shrink down from a giant lake monster to a deer that was a fraction of the size, perhaps it could shrink down even smaller. Small enough to fit inside that tiny little waterhole? Milo was determined to find out.

"PHEW-EEEE-OOO!" Milo whistled to announce his presence. He didn't want to scare it off this time.

Unzipping his bag, he took out a paper parcel from Mandy's Candies and tentatively approached the spring. He placed one end of a long rope of red liquorice into the bubbling water and laid the rest on the soil at its edge. Then he added a trail of gumdrops leading all the way up to the graffiti-covered boulder. "PHEW-EEEE-OOO." Milo set his bag beside the rock and waited.

There was nothing at first. *Is it in there?*

"PHEW-EEEE-OOO," he whistled again.

The liquorice twitched. Milo perked up. All at once the red candy rope disappeared into the simmering spring. *It's working.*

Slowly, snakily, a thin black tendril emerged from the water and felt around in the dirt. *Yikes!* Milo ducked behind the boulder, his instincts urging him to run. *That thing is like a slimy rat tail.* Heart racing, he forced himself to look.

The slithering appendage was exploring the sugary surface of the nearest gumdrop. Another tendril emerged from the spring and groped around, looking for more. As soon as it found the second gumdrop, more dark feelers emerged, resembling the spines of a sea urchin. With a series of SLURPs, the spines clumped together and coagulated to form three fat tentacles, like the ones that had harassed Milo's sinking boat.

Sweet Cerberus.

Bit by bit, a quivering, bulbous, beach ball-sized blob that looked like it was made of inky jello squished up and out of the spring.

Horrified, Milo darted back behind the boulder. *Is* that *what the Thing looks like when it's not pretending to be something else? It's astonishingly gross.* He could hear the creature squidging over pebbles and pine needles, inching ever closer to the boulder. Milo felt the sting of sweat on his brow. Did it know he was there?

"PHBEEWWW-BEEEEEEE-BWOOOO," came an unearthly trill, somehow originating from the blobby Thing.

Milo felt a jolt of prideful recognition. *That's my whistle!* Could it be that the creature was calling to him? He hesitated, not yet willing to emerge from his hiding spot.

Tentatively, a black protrusion groped round

the boulder and found Milo's sleeve. Both he and the Thing flinched, then froze.

Moments passed, Milo hardly daring to breathe. Eventually, the tentacle quietly slithered back to the other side of the boulder. There was a gurgling, sucking sound. Milo could feel all the air in the vicinity rush towards the Thing. What was happening? Digging his nails into his palms, Milo stuck his head round the stone and dared to look.

The creature's gelatinous dark body was growing, narrowing and twisting, like an enormous slab of black clay being moulded from within. Its colour began to pale, turning grey, then bone white. At last, the being congealed and settled into the form of a mighty stag as big as a horse. Colourless slime shimmered on its flanks.

Milo covered his mouth to suppress a squeak.

The horned deer stared down at him, its chestnut eyes mirroring Milo's own apprehension.

Milo reached into his coat pocket and retrieved a large swirly rainbow lollipop. He held it out timorously.

The deer sniffed the treat, then skipped excitedly, sending Milo's pulse skyrocketing. Tentatively, the deer bent down to take the candy, but it changed its mind and sashayed backwards.

"It's okay," Milo assured it. "I won't bite." He was far from certain that the Thing could offer the same guarantee.

Using all the willpower he could muster, Milo sidestepped towards the enormous creature, the candy extended as far as he could reach. "PHEW-EEEE-OOO," he whistled.

Still apprehensive, the deer nipped the head of the lollipop from Milo's hand, crunching its prize as it retreated to the other side of the clearing.

"I'm Milo." Milo pointed to himself. "Is that where you live?" He pointed to the spring.

The creature cocked its head, as if trying to

understand the words. *Can it?* It swallowed the last of the lollipop, then snorted and skipped like a playful puppy.

Milo laughed for what felt like the first time in ages. "You want more, do you?" He took out another lollipop from his pocket and the deer danced in a circle, its formidable antlers whizzing perilously within range of Milo's face.

"Gah!" Milo stumbled back.

Worried the Thing might accidentally trample him, he tossed the lollipop in the air. The Thing reared up and caught the candy in its massive jaws, its front hooves flailing. Landing with a THUD, it looked down to find Milo cowering at the base of the boulder, his arms shielding his head.

From between his elbows Milo watched as the deer finished its sugary treat. And then something changed.

Milo rubbed his eyes, thinking his vision had gone blurry, but there was nothing wrong with his sight. Each hair on the creature's body was vibrating as its form shimmered into translucence. Beads of slimy sweat coursed down its neck and legs as the stag, antlers and all, decreased in size until it was about as tall as Lucy's wolfhound, Errol. When it finished, solidifying once again, it snorted as if to say, "Is this better?"

Dumbfounded, Milo scrambled to his feet. "Thank you. This is a much more manageable size."

Seeming quite proud of itself, the dog-sized deer pranced around, kicking its knees up like a show pony.

Milo laughed. "I think you deserve some more candy, you silly Thingus." Grinning, he disappeared behind the boulder and rummaged through his pack, picking through colourful stretches of taffy, candy buttons, and peppermint patties the size of hockey pucks. When he re-emerged, he stopped in his tracks. "What the—" The peppermint patty he was carrying dropped to the dirt with a THOD.

The creature had mutated again. Well, not the entire creature. Its body was still a graceful, if comically proportioned, white stag. Its head, however…

"How in the world?" Milo found himself looking into a pair of familiar blue eyes.

The Thing's head, while still crowned by a gorgeous spread of antlers, had shrunk and rounded to form a human face, the proportion and colouring of which resembled a somewhat pinched sculpture of Milo himself.

"Holy—" Milo began.

"Holy mother of fewmet flinging frogspit!" interrupted a new voice.

Milo whipped round to find none other than Lucy Sladan gawping at the scene, her mouth open so wide he could see her tonsils.

CHAPTER 14

Remedial Rendezvous

Lucy pushed through the pine branches she'd been crouching behind, heedless of the fact that her parka was covered with black streaks of sticky sap. Her blood bubbled with a confluence of competing emotions.

"I've spent my entire life trying to discover unknown cryptozoological species, and you manage to stumble upon one in a couple of *WEEKS*?!" The last word came out as a shriek.

The human-faced stag reared back on its hind legs.

"Whoa, Thingus." Milo held up his hands to calm the bizarre being. "What are you doing here?" he demanded of Lucy.

"I was gonna ask you the same question." Lucy goggled at the incredible creature. "But now I understand perfectly."

It had taken several hours of intense ingenuity for Lucy to get to the Siren's Lair. She'd spent all morning straddling a cardboard platform tied to two freshly inflated inner tubes, using a tree branch as an oar. Her jeans were wet to the knee. Her teeth chattered in the Autumn wind and strands of sweaty hair clung to her forehead. But none of that mattered right now. What did matter was the magnificent creature before her, which was the most hideously beautiful thing she'd ever seen.

"How could you not tell me about this?"

"Can you keep your voice down?" Milo fumed.

The dog-sized, child-faced deer shifted its weight uneasily from one hoof to the other.

Milo retrieved a chocolate disc from the ground then gently approached the creature. "It's a peppermint patty," he said. "Go on, eat it. It's good."

Keeping its eyes on Lucy, the being plucked the candy from Milo's hand with its human teeth. It dropped the treat on the ground a yard away and munched on it like it was a patch of grass. When it finished, the Thing waggled its antlers happily, its cherubic cheeks covered in chocolate.

"This is so cool!" Lucy chirped. She made a beeline towards the strange being. The creature jumped in alarm and darted behind Milo.

"What are you doing, crazy?" Milo hissed at Lucy. "I've spent over a week gaining this Thing's trust. You're either going to scare it away or it'll rip your face off. You don't know what it's capable of."

"What do you mean?" Lucy could barely rein in her exuberance. "It looks harmless."

"Harmless?" scoffed Milo. "It's a deer with a human face!"

"I know! Isn't it great?"

Milo glared at her, arms crossed.

"Okay. I'll be careful." She rolled her eyes.

With her hand outstretched, Lucy approached the Thing slowly, as she would a stray dog. The being gingerly sniffed her fingers and didn't retreat. With a pointed look at Milo, Lucy gently patted the creature's shoulder. She could feel a soft purr deep within its throat. Scratching up its neck, she felt under its chin. The skin on its face was as soft as a baby's. "This is incredible," she marvelled.

"Will you please go home?" Milo sulked. "This is *my* cryptozoological creature, not yours."

Lucy laughed. "Fat chance, fancy-pants."

"How did you find me, anyway?"

"I saw your big red kayak."

Milo slumped. "It was that easy?"

"I thought you were sneaking out here to feed a den of stranded bear cubs or something, but this..." Lucy laughed as the strange being nosed Milo's pockets with its freaky face. "What is this magnificent weirdo? It looks like some kind of

Egyptian god. Maybe it's a sphinx..."

"A sphinx has a human head," said Milo, "but with the body of a lion, not a deer."

Lucy looked at him sideways. "How do you know that?"

"You're not the only one well versed in mythical creatures." Milo smugly lifted his chin.

"Is that so, Smarty McFly?" Lucy retrieved her notebook from her pocket and prepared to take notes. "So what is it, then?"

"I have no idea," Milo admitted. "As far as I can tell, he's unlike any known cryptozoological specimen."

"He? How do you know the creature's a boy?"

"Well, he's got antlers, doesn't he?"

"Fair enough."

The child-faced deer nibbled at Milo's pocket and nudged his shoulder with an antler.

"Ow." Milo held up his hand. "Stop that."

The creature stomped his hoof, as if asking Milo where the candy was and why wasn't he giving him more candy right now.

"You need to be patient, Thingus," said Milo, hands on his hips.

Huffily, the creature trotted over to the hot spring, shot an annoyed pout over his shoulder, then shuddered and jellified into a blob of black goo, draining his mass into the bubbling waters in a matter of seconds.

Lucy dropped her notebook. "He's a shapeshifter!" she squealed. "Just like the others! This is— Wait," she said. "You discovered a member of an entirely new species and you named him 'Thingus'?"

"It was the only name I could— Others?" Milo's mode switched from annoyance to intense interest. "What do you mean, others?"

Oh snap. Lucy couldn't reveal what she knew about the Pretenders without putting them in danger, but she wanted to share the Truth so badly it hurt. Was she going to have to lie to Milo yet again? "I mean," she said, choosing her words carefully, "like those people who turned into Bigwoofs."

"That's just what I was thinking!" Milo exclaimed, his cheeks rosy in the chill air. "But Thingus is different. His transformations aren't happening *to* him. He decides how to change, and when. It's totally incredible, isn't it?"

"Totally." Lucy picked her notebook up out of the mud, thoughts colliding in her brain a mile a minute. *Thingus is a Pretender. He has to be!*

She listened keenly as Milo described in detail how Thingus had morphed from a giant tentacled lake monster into a white stag, and the disgusting amount of slime his transformation entailed.

Slime is basically Pretender juice! "He had tentacles, you say?" Lucy jotted down a few key words: "Sharkosquidosaurus!?" "Stag", "Doggydeerboy". "Has Thingus ever turned into a human?" she asked.

"Not unless you count the strange face he had today."

Lucy chewed the inside of her cheeks, thinking. "Can you get him to come back out of the spring?"

"I can try."

Milo retrieved a bag of peanut brittle, tossed a few pieces into the burbling water and whistled. A moment later, a slimy tentacle emerged.

Lucy watched, hypnotised, as the slippery creature flubbered out of the spring. She felt a breeze as the gooey Thing doubled, then tripled in size, sucking in air as he grew. The formless being lengthened, its saggy middle rising and dividing to form a torso with four spindly legs. A protrusion at the top of his body stretched out and upwards into a mammalian neck and head, from which two bony antlers emerged. The shiny black creature turned matte and white fur flashed across the now solid surface of its skin. Once again, the Thing had adopted the form of a small stag, without the human features.

"Holy crudberries," Lucy murmured.

Milo fed the Thing another piece of peanut brittle.

"Please tell me you have video footage of this,"

said Lucy.

"No way," said Milo. "I'm all out of cameras, and my phone's not secure. I don't want my dad to know about Thingus yet. He's not ready."

"You're hiding this discovery from your dad?"

"I don't want to talk about it," Milo muttered.

"Wow," said Lucy, impressed. She sketched a likeness of Milo's description of the lake monster. "Is this what the tentacles looked like, or should they be 'snakier'?" She held up her notebook to show Milo the drawing. For the first time Lucy noticed the graffiti-covered boulder behind him. *No. Flippin. Way.* "It's the symbols!"

Running over to the massive rock, she looked past the spray-painted names and profanities and focused on the markings carved into the stone itself. She ran her fingers across time-worn rows of engraved shapes, dots, lines and squiggles. *How long have these been here? Decades? Centuries?*

Milo peered over her shoulder as Thingus danced in circles, begging for more candy.

"Just a minute, Thingus," said Milo. "What is it?" he asked Lucy.

She showed him the glyphs in Willow's notebook. "I've seen symbols like these before, under the Nu Co. factory."

"Under?" Milo ran his fingers along the boulder's engraved surface. "What language is it?"

"I don't know," said Lucy, "but I'm pretty sure I know someone who does."

"Who?"

Thingus snorted to get their attention to no avail.

Lucy squinched her face. "You're not gonna like it." A gust of cold air sent a shiver down her spine.

Milo's eyes narrowed with understanding. "You mean my father, don't you?"

"Well, I— Sufferin' slugspit!" Lucy pointed behind Milo.

"What?" He spun round.

The stag had mutated again. His body now

glittered with silver opalescence. A flowing mane, every colour of the rainbow, ran along his head and neck. Instead of antlers, there was a single horn on his forehead that glowed with soft white light.

Lucy looked down at the cover of Willow's notebook, which featured a metallic illustration of a unicorn. "It's just like the picture." She gazed, awestruck, at Thingus. "You're pretty smart, aren't you?"

The unicorn reared up proudly on its hind legs, its prismatic mane fluttering in the wind. Lucy took care to stay out of range of its silver hooves.

"PHBEEWWW-BEEEEEEE-BWOOOO!"

"Did he just purse his horsey lips and whistle?" asked Lucy, agog.

"I think he wants more candy," Milo gulped. He ran behind the boulder and returned with a giant wheel of black liquorice. He tossed it high and the unicorn caught it in mid-air.

Thingus took one bite, then emitted a high-pitched multi-tonal scream. The kids covered their ears and huddled together as the creature collapsed in on itself, morphing into a writhing knot of angry tentacles. Reaching for the hot spring, the Thing squelched his wormy mass into the steaming hole until all that was left was a trail of transparent sluggish slime and a tooth-marked wheel of uneaten candy.

Lucy uncovered her ears, staring incredulously at a wide-eyed, unblinking Milo. "Dude." She shook her head. "Nobody likes black liquorice."

CHAPTER 15

Burger Burglar

The jukebox at Buck's Burger Barn kicked out a twangy country song. Milo watched, fascinated, as Lucy took a big slurp of her mint milkshake. It was green, and not because it was infused with a healthy dose of kale.

"I can't believe you've never been here before," said Lucy, a dab of whipped cream on the tip of her nose. "This is the best restaurant in Sticky Pines."

Milo sipped his iced tea and took in the barnyard decor. *This place looks like a scarecrow's fever dream.* "We usually eat in."

"Order something." Lucy pushed the menu

towards him. "You need to eat. You did all the rowing."

Milo had offered Lucy a lift to shore in his kayak, as the inner-tube contraption she'd lashed together had more or less disintegrated by the time she'd reached the island.

The kayak was just big enough for both of them to squeeze into and, with only one paddle, Milo had to row twice the weight he was used to. Sitting in the restaurant two hours later, he could feel his biceps burning. *I'll need a long Epsom-salt bath tonight.*

"Why don't you try a burger?" Lucy pointed to one titled the "Howdy Doody Double-Decker". She leaned in. "I'd skip the hot dogs."

"Burger it is."

The gingham-clad waitress approached, chewing gum and playing with a pigtail. Her nametag read: MICHELLE.

"May I have one of these?" Milo pointed to the "Howdy Doody" on the menu rather than saying it out loud. "Medium rare, please."

Michelle scratched her nose with her pen. "I'll be honest, kid, Bernard's just gonna cook it how he's gonna cook it."

"I'll trust the judgement of the chef." Milo smiled tightly.

"Rings or fries?" asked Michelle.

"Rings."

Lucy held up a hand. "Those're too greasy for your sophisticated taste buds. If I may?"

Milo shrugged.

"He'll have the sweet potato fries. And I'd like a grilled cheese with all the fixin's, please."

"You got it." Michelle winked at Lucy. "Tell your folks I say hi."

"Will do." Lucy gave her a thumbs-up.

Michelle sauntered off to the next table. It was early evening and the restaurant was filling up with the Saturday-night crowd. Milo had yet to experience the local nightlife, but he suspected things could get rowdy.

"Sweet potatoes are yams, right?" he asked.

"Forget the yams," said Lucy. "We need to plan."

"We? Who said there's a we? You lied at the factory, and I still don't know if I can trust you."

"I didn't *want* to lie." Lucy looked like a cat caught eating the Christmas goose. "It's all so confusing. This fight between us has been killing me, Fish. You don't even know."

"I do know. It's been killing me, too."

"I hope..." Lucy seemed to be fighting the urge to say something. "I hope someday you'll understand why I did what I did."

Milo sighed. *She sounds exactly like my father.*

"I just want us to be friends again," said Lucy.

"Well." Milo stirred the ice in his tea. "I'm here."

"That's a start," said Lucy. "Let's shake on it."

Milo held out a hand. Instead of taking it, Lucy tossed him a straw from the dispenser on the table. She gestured for him to drink from the thick green milkshake.

Together, they sipped from their straws. Milo

was certain the shake would taste like toothpaste, but it was creamy with just a hint of mint.

"That's utterly delicious," he said.

"You can have the rest." Lucy passed it over. "You've earned it."

Milo hadn't realised just how hungry he was. He sucked down the shake until he felt a searing pain behind his eyes.

"Oh dear," he winced.

"Brain freeze." Lucy burst out laughing.

Michelle came by with two steaming plates and slid them on the table. Unable to control himself, Milo started eating before Lucy's plate had even touched down. The sweet potato fries were heavenly. *This place isn't bad at all. My dad said there'd be nothing but salmonella on the menu.*

"So." Lucy splurted some mayonnaise and ketchup on to her plate. "If we wanna know what Thingus is and where he comes from, we need to translate the symbols on that stone."

Milo bit into his burger, which was, thankfully, cooked medium rather than well done. "And how are we supposed to do that?"

"Well…" Lucy gripped her sandwich. "There's one person I can think of who's translated symbols like that before."

Milo frowned. "No."

"C'mon, Fish. I'll bet a smart guy like you knows exactly where his dad keeps important documents and such."

Milo thought of his father's high-tech briefcase and its mysterious contents. *I wonder if…* He banished the thought. "No!"

Lucy tried to catch his eye. "It's all in service of the Truth."

"Look," he said, "I want to learn about Thingus as much as you do, but what you're asking for is impossible. And, what's more, I wouldn't do it even if I could. He's my father. It would be a supreme violation of his privacy. End of story."

"Fish."

"Lucy."

She looked at him forlornly with large doe

eyes, magnified by her glasses.

"I told you," he snapped, "I won't do it."

Milo stifled a yawn as he sat in bed, staring at the clock on his bedroom wall. His dad had gone to bed an hour ago. By now he should be fast asleep. The clock struck two. Milo's head fell into his hands. *Fie on Lucy Sladan and her endless stream of insane yet compelling ideas.*

Dressed all in black, Milo pulled his turtleneck over the lower half of his face, then tiptoed across the hallway and down the stairs. At last, he reached the door to the master bathroom, which connected to his father's bedroom through a large walk-in closet.

He paused, his sweaty hand resting on the doorknob. What would happen if he got caught? *I'll probably get sent to boarding school.* What would happen if he turned back? *I'll never learn the truth about Thingus.* Which option was worse?

Resigned, he opened the bathroom door. The

dim glow of his phone screen illuminated the way past a trio of glass sinks, a Japanese toilet that squirted water, a stone-tiled rainfall shower, and a large egg-shaped bathtub. Finally, Milo reached the second door.

He opened it without a squeak, revealing a walk-in closet the size of Lucy's bedroom. His father's crisply pressed suits, ties and dress shirts hung on the left. On the right were his stepmother's designer dresses, handbags and rows upon rows of shoes. Milo crept along until he reached the bedroom door, his father's saw-like snores rumbling faintly on the other side. *How thoughtful of nature to provide a sound effect to let you know when someone is not conscious.*

Cautiously, Milo stuck his head into the room, his eyes landing on the king-sized bed on the other side. Neither his father nor his stepmother stirred. *So far so good. Now where's that briefcase?*

The cavernous swan-white bedroom was impeccably tidy. Floor-to-ceiling windows overlooked the forest. Instead of curtains, the glass dimmed itself automatically at night. Milo could barely make out the shape of the moon, half full and high in the night sky.

He silently made his way across the sheepskin rug. Mr Fisher lay on his back, his mouth open, his eyes darting around under closed lids. *He's probably dreaming about work.* Kaitlyn lay on the other side, face down, her platinum hair tousled over a silk pillowcase.

Milo dropped to his knees and peered under the bed. *Oho, there it is!* The briefcase was exactly where he thought it would be. *Milo Fisher, do you know your father or what?* He slid it out and set it at his side. At any moment he was going to have to move, and fast. Now came the hard, nay, the *impossible* part. Getting the code from his dad's watch without waking him up.

Fearing he'd lose his nerve, Milo gently lifted the grey duvet. His father's chest rose and fell steadily, his arms crossed over his midsection. The two watches were stacked one against the other on his left wrist. Milo strained to see the code, but it was too dark. *There must be a light on that thing*. Holding his breath, he reached out to press the button on the watch.

His fingers were mere millimetres away when Mr Fisher's snore caught in his throat and turned into a cough. He stirred. Dismayed, Milo pancaked to the floor and slid under the bed. He waited, his heart pounding in his ears and rug burns stinging his elbows. Finally, his father rolled over, muttering something about "bonds". His arm fell over the side of the bed.

Mr Fisher's wrist dangled just above Milo's head. As soon as the snores returned at regular intervals, Milo counted to three, then, careful not to touch his father's skin, pressed a button on the side of the not-watch. The face lit up in ghostly green, displaying a string of seven numbers. *The code changes every thirty seconds*, Milo remembered. *How long does this one have left?* Just then, the numbers switched.

Milo rolled out from under the bed, arching away from his father's hand, repeating the numbers in his head. *6-3-8-9-0-4-7, 6-3-8-9-0-4-7…* He snatched up the briefcase and raced quietly over to the walk-in closet, silently shutting the door behind him. How much time had elapsed already? Ten seconds? Twenty? He knelt by a shoe rack and pulled out his phone, fumbling with it until the flashlight turned on.

He punched the numbers into the interface. 6-3-8-9-0…

Oh no. What are the last two? Milo was pretty sure the next number was 4, which he pressed, but was the one after a 2 or a 7? *I should have written it down! I'm not cut out for a life of crime.* His time was nearly up, and may have run out already. Flipping a coin in his head, he punched the number 7 on to the keypad. With a mechanical BEEP the briefcase unlocked. *Huzzah!*

Had anyone heard? He pressed his ear to the door. Nothing. Time to see what was inside.

The briefcase's contents were mostly documents. Milo rifled through a stack of manila folders, reading the typewritten headline on each tab: "Hypothetical Taxonomy of Preternatural Organisms", "SP Biological Subversives", "Deviant Biochemical Susceptibilities". *Holy cow.* Milo wasn't sure what all of those words meant, but he knew that Lucy's glasses would melt off her face if she ever saw them.

Tempted as he was to read it all, Milo had struck a bargain with himself: he would look for the key to the symbols, which was precisely what Lucy had asked for, but he wouldn't invade his father's privacy any further, NO MATTER WHAT HE SAW. Frankly, he wished he hadn't seen this much.

He flipped through until he found one titled: "Compendium of Preternatural Linguistic Symbology". *Symbology. Symbols!* This was it. He pulled out the folder. Inside were dozens of handwritten pages, all filled with bizarre-looking letters, phrases and their English translations. *Bingo Thingo.*

Silently, Milo snapped picture after picture

with his phone, mentally patting himself on the back after each one. He was just photographing the last page when he heard the sound of a knee bumping into a side table. "Oof. Owie."

Kaitlyn was awake. *Oh no. Oh no, no, no…*

Milo shoved the folder back in its place and closed the case as quietly as he could. He dived into a densely packed rack of clothes and hid behind a sparkly blue gown covered in sequins and a white fur coat that smelled like dog. He hugged the case and tried not to breathe too loudly, which inevitably made him feel like he was suffocating.

Kaitlyn stumbled through the closet on her way to the bathroom, her silk floral pyjamas brushing against Milo's hiding place. She flipped on the bathroom light and, mercifully, shut the door behind her.

Milo's nerves crackled with anxiety. What should he do? Stay put? Sneak out through the bedroom door? *Bad idea. Dad might have woken up, too.* Visions of his father's reaction to his only son's betrayal spun through Milo's head. Worse, he felt a tickle on his nose. He was going to sneeze. *What is this ridiculous coat made of?!*

The toilet flushed. *Oh please, not now.* Milo held his breath and plugged his nose as Kaitlyn opened the door.

Just then, Milo's phone began to buzz. *NOOOO!* The vibrations echoed around the room. *Who could be calling now?* He fumbled with the device but couldn't find the button to stop the call. Fingers sweaty, he pressed everything until the buzzing stopped.

Kaitlyn turned on the light.

Hardly risking a movement, Milo checked the screen to see who might have brought on his untimely demise. "Sladan Home", it read. *Lucy. Of course.* She must have stayed up to find out how his ill-conceived caper had gone. He wondered if she'd attend his funeral.

His stepmother's footsteps drew nearer.

Should he surrender now? Maybe he could pretend he was sleepwalking or had recently developed an obsession with sequins? Milo peeked through the garments.

Hand on her hip, Kaitlyn turned towards the hanging dresses. Milo braced himself for the inevitable scream. It never came. Kaitlyn turned the other way, then back again. She was looking at herself in the full-length mirror on the bathroom door. Something orange was sticking out of her ear.

Earplugs! Milo exhaled a whirligig of relief. *She wears earplugs because of Dad's snoring!* Milo had never been so grateful for his father's noisy medical condition.

Kaitlyn yawned, flicked off the light and returned to bed, leaving the closet door open. After a brief pause, Mr Fisher's snores resumed.

Milo emailed Lucy as he waited for Kaitlyn to fall asleep. "GO TO BED," he typed. "It's done. I'll show you everything tomorrow."

He hit send, then exited his hiding place. Careful as a contortionist on a high wire, Milo returned the briefcase to the exact spot he'd found it, then slipped through the closet and out the bathroom door. Once in the hallway, he raced back to his room and hopped into bed, panting.

The phone buzzed in his pocket. It was Lucy. Her message contained nothing but twelve thumbs-up emojis followed by six exclamation marks.

Milo replied with a smiley face.

CHAPTER 16

The Siren Stone

"I got another one!" Lucy exclaimed triumphantly. She bundled Milo's printed compendium under her arm and scribbled the definition to the symbol she'd just translated. After many hours of work, she had nearly finished deciphering all of the mysterious glyphs on the "Siren Stone", as she'd christened the graffitied boulder.

Milo was sat cross-legged on the ground next to Thingus, who was waddling around in the form of a seabird with massive grey wings.

When the kids had arrived at the island that morning, Thingus had appeared as a white stag and greeted them with an enthusiastic prance. Milo, using more of Millepoids's candy, had spent the day coaxing the creature to shrink down smaller and smaller until he spontaneously morphed into an albatross. The ease with which he transformed suggested he had adopted this shape before.

Lucy pointed to a spot on the boulder. "These four symbols say: 'Crawl. Swim. Fly. Stand.'"

"Huh," said Milo. "Is that a sentence?"

Lucy double-checked her translation. The symbol key from Mr Fisher's briefcase contained an incredible assortment of hand-drawn glyphs, each accompanied by a definition. "Maybe it's like, a list of all the stuff Thingus can do?" she ventured.

Milo curled his lip sceptically. "Well, he can crawl, swim and walk. Watch this, though."

He tossed a gumdrop high into the air. The albatross jumped, flapping its massive wings clumsily before face-planting in the mud.

"See?" said Milo. "He can't fly."

With dirt caked on his orange beak Thingus scrabbled across the clearing and pecked the gumdrop out from under a bush.

Lucy laughed. She couldn't remember ever having felt more alive; she was currently probing beyond the boundaries of the unknown in the presence of another actual person who not only believed the things she was saying, but who was PHYSICALLY INTERACTING WITH A MIRACULOUS CRYPTOZOOLOGICAL SPECIMEN RIGHT BEFORE HER EYES. Had she died and gone to heaven? *Today* – Lucy inhaled the freshest air she had ever tasted – *anything is possible.* If only she could tell Milo the Truth about the Pretenders, it would all be perfect.

Milo crawled over and scratched the shapeshifter between his useless wings. "I wonder if there are any more creatures like Thingus? I'd hate to think he was all alone in the world."

"That is an interesting question," said Lucy,

heat flooding to her cheeks.

"I was thinking," said Milo. "Based on how the glyphs on the stone have worn away over time, these symbols could be old." He lured Thingus closer with a chocolate button. "*Really* old."

"You might be on to something there," said Lucy, thinking of the hundred-year-old yearbook photos of the Other Mrs Stricks and Alastair Chelon.

Who had created these glyphs, and why? Was it the Pretenders? If not them, who? After all, the symbols under the factory had spelled out the warning "Beware the Pretenders". Why would they create a warning about themselves? What did it mean? It would be so much easier to figure all this out if she could just discuss it with Milo. *I can trust him, can't I? But I definitely can't trust his dad. Ugh, why can't he be an orphan?*

Lucy returned her attention to the Siren Stone. "Ooh, this circle with a dot in the middle means 'lake'."

Thingus looked up from the pile of chocolate he was munching on, his feathered tail twitching. Lucy blinked. Was she imagining things, or was the creature listening to her? He fluffed out his feathers and went back to his favourite pastime: eating.

"Hey, you," said Lucy. Thingus continued gorging himself with gusto. "Refrigerator," she said. "Crudberries." The bird ignored her. "Thingus." The creature stopped and looked up. "I think he knows his name," she gawped.

"I told you he was smart," Milo grinned. "Aren't you, you little genius?" He tickled Thingus's tummy and the albatross leaned in with pleasure. A sound escaped his beak that was halfway between a bird's titter and a child's laugh.

"That laugh is creepy, though," said Lucy.

Milo tsked. "I can't believe you of all people would call an amazing supernatural being 'creepy'. He's not creepy; he's cute."

"What I can't believe is that he decided to turn

into a bird when he could easily be a Pegasus or a centaur."

"Well, I'm hoping he'll stick with being a cute animal when I show him to my dad," said Milo. "That way, he'll know Thingus isn't dangerous."

"*What?*" Lucy dropped her notebook. "You're going to show Thingus to your father? Are you insane?"

Milo frowned. "He'll find out eventually. Believe me."

Lucy did believe him. To her everlasting annoyance, Mr Fisher had been the first to discover the mysterious shapeshifters of Sticky Pines. But the only thing he could think to do with this mind-blowing information was to root out, dissect and destroy them. *He's not wrong about what they are; he's just a dillweed.* If Fisher found out about Thingus, there was no telling what he'd do. There was still time to persuade Milo not to tell his father about their discovery, but she'd have to tread carefully.

"Okay –" Lucy picked up where she had left

off in her translation – "these next symbols mean something like 'with two-footed locomotion, balance with the head'." She scratched her nose under her glasses. "Are these tips on how to walk like a person?"

"Or a bird?" said Milo.

"Good point," said Lucy, writing that down. "I wonder if this rock is a giant instruction manual…"

"An instruction manual for whom?"

"For Thingus," *And the other Pretenders like him.* "Do you think he can read?"

"Now that would be something."

Milo shook the bag of candies like a maraca, then patted his shoulder. The creature barrelled towards him and tried to scramble up Milo's legs, his wings flailing.

"No," Milo laughed. "You need to *fly* up. That's what your wings are for." The awkward albatross pecked at Milo's shoelace like it was a worm.

"Finished!" Lucy set down the compendium

with a flourish.

"Well?" Milo cradled Thingus to his chest.

"Ahem. The Siren Stone says: 'Welcome, Hidden Wanderer, to the Water of Life. This is your place of existence for many suns. In the lake and on the island, you will learn. You will extend. You will transmute. You will become. Crawl. Swim. Fly. Stand. Dance. Be. But a warning: do not leave the lake, do not leave the island, until you master your forms. The key to Becoming is Understanding. Hide from that which you cannot Become. Become only what you can befriend. To Dominate is to Overtake. Remember: you are never alone. Never far from home. Always Protected. If Those Who Dominate overwhelm, sound the Siren. Welcome, Hidden Wanderer, to your new home.'"

"Wow." Milo read it all again over Lucy's shoulder. "What does it mean?"

It means that this is where all the Pretenders came from. Right here, in the middle of Black Hole Lake. Lucy tried to envision Mrs Stricks squeezing out of the hot spring like blubbery black toothpaste from a tube. She shuddered.

"It means that this area is like a training ground where they can learn how to take new forms," she said.

"They?"

"I mean, Thingus," Lucy corrected herself. "The royal 'they'."

"So Thingus *can* read?"

"Presumably."

Thingus squawked.

"All right, buddy," said Milo, "if you're smart enough to read, you can definitely learn to fly." He held out his arms and flapped to demonstrate.

Thingus hopped and copied Milo's action. He fluttered his wings and ran across the clearing, remaining disappointingly earthbound.

Milo picked up the floundering bird, wings flapping against his face, and set him on top of the boulder. The boy took a few steps back and held out his hands. "Jump," he commanded.

Thingus shuffled uncertainly to the boulder's

edge. He prepared to jump, then changed his mind and retreated to the centre of the boulder, burying his head under his wing.

Out of the corner of her eye, Lucy spotted a dark speck hovering high above the treetops. When she turned to look, it darted off, disappearing from view in an instant. *Is that what I think it is?* "Um, Milo?"

"Yeah?" Resignedly, Milo set Thingus safely on the ground.

"I think I just saw a Nu Co. surveillance drone."

Milo paled. "Where?"

Crashing through spiny briars and low pine branches, they rushed out to the shore and scoured the sky for any sign of a drone, but they saw nothing but a pair of Canada geese flying across the clouds.

"Say it was a drone," said Lucy. "What would it have seen? Just us playing with a bird, right?"

"Right," said Milo. "I'm sure it was nothing, anyway." He looked far from certain.

Lucy checked her watch. "It's time to go home, anyway."

They bid farewell to Thingus, stuffed their things into the kayak, and took off across the lake, gliding under the sunset in thoughtful silence. Back ashore, they hopped on their bikes.

"I'll see you at school," Milo called over his shoulder.

"We saved your spot at the lunch table," Lucy yelled back.

It had been the best day Lucy had ever spent. So why did she have a nagging sense of impending doom?

CHAPTER 17

Lars Supper

Milo was buzzing as he wound his way through the crowded school cafeteria. Life was finally returning to normal. All it had taken was the discovery of an otherworldly monster with unfathomable powers. *But I guess, in Sticky Pines, that's as normal as one might hope for.*

"Are my eyes deceiving me?" Tex embraced Milo at their usual table at the back of the canteen. "Welcome home, Feesh!"

Milo ceremoniously took his seat across from Lucy, who looked as happy as a pig in a puddle. He unpacked his feta and lentil salad, which struck him as underwhelming for such a celebratory occasion. Maybe after school they could stop by that hokey burger joint again. He was craving another mint milkshake. And those sweet potato fries…

Lucy ripped open a packet of hot sauce and squeezed it over her plateful of tacos. "Want one?" she offered her tray to Milo.

"Thanks." He eagerly nabbed a taco. The hot sauce burned his tongue, but the taco was one of the best things he'd ever tasted. *Am I going nuts or is this wackadoodle mountain town growing on me?*

"Sladan!" called a strident voice from across the room.

Lucy jumped in her seat. "What did I do?"

A slender girl with short dark hair and a yellow blazer strode across the cafeteria.

"You had a deadline this morning, did you not?" Tex whispered. He cradled his head in his hands.

The girl stopped in front of their table, her arms crossed. Milo noticed that she had a nose ring. He'd never seen one in person before.

"Where's my article?" the girl demanded.

"Oh, snap, the deadline," said Lucy.

"Milo Fisher, have you met Gertie Lee?" Tex introduced them. "She is the editor of the *SPEAMS Sentinel.*"

Milo held out his hand, which Gertie shook harder than necessary.

Without letting go she turned to Lucy. "Dining with the enemy, I see?"

"Enemy?" Milo pulled his hand free.

"No offence," said Gertie, "but your father's company is nothing but a force of destruction and despair. The world needs to retain its temperate rain forests, thank you very much."

Tex shrugged apologetically at Milo, who was at a loss for words.

"And speaking of Nu Co. –" Gertie turned to Lucy – "what did your investigation uncover?"

"You're writing about my dad's company?" asked Milo.

"It's *my* dad's company, too," Lucy responded,

avoiding eye contact.

Milo felt the sting of annoyance. Why was every aspect of his life now tainted by his father's business affairs? This was not an issue most thirteen-year-olds had to navigate.

"We go to print at the end of the week," said Gertie. "I've made space for you on the front page, Sladan. You've got two days to turn in your piece, and it had better be good, and I mean polished like a diamond tiara, or your journalistic credibility is dust."

Milo had the impression that Ms Lee was a girl with a frighteningly bright future ahead of her.

"Understood." Lucy sheepishly saluted.

"Gertie," said Tex. He reclined, one arm dangling suavely over the back of his chair. "Did you see my latest satire on the school's paltry response to the climate crisis?"

"I did, indeed," said Gertie. "Really good stuff, Arkhipov. You're a go-getter. I like it. I wish some of that gusto would rub off on your slacker friend, here."

Lucy leaned back peevishly.

Tex rose and offered his arm to Gertie. "May I explain the symbolism of the frog in boiling water as I escort you to the boiler room?"

She linked her elbow with his. "You know," she said as they sauntered off, "you've got an intriguingly dark sense of humour."

"As they say in Russia, it is better to laugh than to cry, since both are useless anyway."

"That's profound, yo."

Tex winked at Lucy as he and Gertie exited the cafeteria, deep in conversation.

Milo blinked. "And I thought I'd seen everything."

"I think he's wearing a freshly ironed pair of jeans today," said Lucy, disturbed.

"So you're writing an expose on Nu Co.?" Milo turned to face her. "Since when?"

"Since you weren't talking to me," she said. "And anyway, something weird *is* going on over there. Everyone's saying so."

"Seems like there's something weird going on everywhere," muttered Milo.

"Welcome to Sladanville, my friend."

Milo laughed. "Speaking of strange places," he said, lowering his voice, "how many shapeshifters like Thingus do you think there are in Sticky Pines?"

Lucy choked on her food and started coughing.

"If you think about it," Milo continued, "they could be anywhere, right? They could be anyTHING."

Nodding, Lucy took a sip of water.

Milo gasped as something occurred to him. "What if there are Thinguses that could actually turn into *people*?"

Lucy coughed so hard she spat water all over the table.

"Are you okay?" Milo hopped up and patted her on the back.

Nanoseconds later, his chair went flying as someone deliberately rammed into it. His backpack was knocked to the floor, its contents spilling out across the linoleum.

"Outta my way, rich boy," said Lars, the hulking seventh-grade bully.

Milo snapped round to face him. "Why don't you watch where you're going, you bug-brained barbarian?" It was by far the rudest thing he had ever said to anyone. For a split second he felt pretty good. Then Lars grabbed him by the collar and pulled him nose to nose. The warmth drained from Milo's face. *Uh-oh.*

"You telling me what to do, fish guts?" snarled Lars. His breath smelled like Cheetos and unbridled rage. "Like your old man does to my ma, keeping her at that stupid factory all day and night, cleaning up his stinking messes?"

The cafeteria fell silent as everyone turned to stare.

"I honestly don't know what you're talking about," said Milo.

Lars pushed him back and Milo stumbled over his social studies book.

"Back off, Lars," Lucy sputtered, still coughing.

"Stay out of it, grape-nut," Lars spat. "What are you gonna do, tell your mommy?"

Lucy shot daggers at Lars as he sidled up to Milo, towering menacingly overhead.

"You and your old man think you can boss everyone around, don't you?"

"I. Uh. No?" said Milo. *Nice going, Fish. That'll teach him.*

Lars yanked Milo off the ground, pulling his collared shirt out of the waistband of his khakis. Toes dangling, Milo realised with a jolt that he'd never been in a physical fight before and he had no idea what to do. His arms and legs felt like wet noodles.

"Is there a problem over there, Mr Darby?" shouted Principal Pakuna from the middle of the cafeteria. The middle-aged ponytailed woman marched towards them, her sleeveless cardigan swinging around her slight frame. She stopped halfway across the room, quietly daring the boys to make her walk all the way over there.

Lars dropped Milo, who felt the shock of the impact rise from his heels to his knees as he landed on the floor.

"No problem." Lars tapped Milo roughly on the arm. "We were just horsing around."

"That's what I thought," said Pakuna, hands on her hips.

Milo seethed as Lars walked off like nothing had happened. Straightening her cardigan, the principal tailed the bully out of the room.

Lucy, finally done coughing, knelt down to help Milo pick up his belongings. "Are you okay?"

He huffily packed away his papers. "Here we are messing around with a cryptozoological oddity, and an oversized twelve-year-old is what makes me almost wet myself." He crumpled his maths homework and shoved it into his pack.

"I could *kill* that fewmet-flinging fool," Lucy snarled. She picked up a small paper rectangle from the floor. "What's this?"

Milo glanced over. "Oh. That." It was the tarot card of the crumbling pyramid. He'd been using it as a bookmark. "I accidentally took it from this weird lady at The Woo Woo Store. Why?"

"Look." Lucy pointed fiercely at the hand-drawn glyphs on the back of the card. "These are the same symbols as on the Siren Stone."

Milo stared in confusion. "They are?"

"Why didn't you mention this before?"

Milo rubbed his neck, still smarting from Lars's grip. "I forgot about it. The woman told me it was just a Sticky Pines thing. Maybe she saw them on the stone and thought they were pretty?"

"Don't you see, Fish?" Lucy's face was so red he was worried her head might explode. "The tarot lady must know something about Thingus, about who made the symbols, about who knows what else? We need to go to The Woo Woo Store. Now."

"But I still have three more classes," said

Milo. He scanned the cafeteria, clocking all the kids who were staring. A table of popular kids he'd thought were friends avoided eye contact when he looked their way. A blonde girl (*what's her name, Amy Something?*), leaned over and whispered something into Joey Peluso's ear, then they both laughed. *Does the whole school hate me?* It was certainly starting to feel like it. *Flip it*. "Yeah, okay," he said. "Let's go."

CHAPTER 18

Demon Deluge

I can't believe Milo may have discovered a WHOLE OTHER Pretender without even realising it! Lucy rode on the back of his bike seat, clinging to his middle as he bobbed up and down, pedalling through the rain while standing up. *If only we'd been* talking *to one another, I could've known about this Marietta Corbin lady weeks ago. How many donkey-kickin' Pretenders live in Sticky Pines, anyway?*

They splashed through a massive puddle as they turned on to Main Street. Lucy was drenched from the waist down, but Milo was wearing a set of yellow rain gear he'd retrieved from his locker that resembled a hazmat suit. It was extraordinarily unattractive but very effective.

"You really think Ms Corbin knows about Thingus?" Milo tossed his oversized hood out of his eyes.

"I'd bet my boots on it," Lucy responded.

They slid to a stop at the corner of Ravenstone Way. Lucy hopped off and jumped across the overflowing gutter while Milo locked his bike to a lamp post.

Lucy had never been in Ms Corbin's boutique before. Mostly because it was called "The Woo Woo Store", and Lucy's skin hurt whenever she encountered 'mystical' mumbo jumbo like that. It was all so boringly human. However, she was now kicking herself for not realising that some of the weirdos in Sticky Pines might actually be, well, weirdos.

The bells on the front door chimed frenetically as Lucy burst through. "Hello?" she called, bumping into a rotating display of dreamcatchers.

Milo caught the stand before it could fall on her. "Calm down," he warned. "People generally don't answer questions after you've demolished their livelihoods."

Be cool, Sladan. Lucy took a deep breath and shook out her hair, which had gone frizzy in the rain. *Marietta Corbin, I predict your future involves answering a slugload of questions.*

Lucy rounded the stand and stopped short. Instead of a woman with red hair, a man in a ruffly white shirt stood behind the shop counter. He was arranging a vase filled with black roses, his fingers adorned with silver rings and blue nail polish. A dark fringe fell jauntily across his forehead. "May I –" he glanced disapprovingly at the puddle gathering at Lucy's feet – "help you?"

"We're looking for—" Lucy slipped in the puddle, splatting on the ground next to a gnome statue.

Milo pulled her up by the sleeve. "Some

supplies," he finished. "For..." He looked to Lucy for help with what could possibly be done with the objects sold in The Woo Woo Store.

"Summoning demons," Lucy offered.

Milo visibly shrank into his raincoat.

"Demons?" The man looked positively appalled.

Huh, thought Lucy. *From the look of it I woulda thought this guy was into that sorta thing.*

Milo laughed loudly. "She's joking." He glared at Lucy. "We were hoping to speak to the lady who works here. She has red hair and reads people's fortunes?"

"I'm afraid Marietta's out acquiring supplies for a private gathering this evening," the man apologised. "You're welcome to browse until she returns. Ouija boards are in the back."

Lucy and Milo strolled stiffly to the rear of the shop, huddling between a bookshelf and a case filled with crystals.

"Can we just come back later?" Milo whispered. "This place creeps me out."

"Maybe that emo guy can give us the address where we can find her." Lucy took out the unicorn notebook and turned to a fresh page.

"Maybe he would have," Milo chided her, "if you hadn't told him we were demon-summoning *warlocks*."

"Warlocks aren't real."

"Neither are transmutational lake monsters –" Milo rapped his knuckles on her notebook – "yet here we are."

The chimes at the front entrance tinkled, followed by the sound of stomping boots. *Marietta Corbin?*

Lucy and Milo peeked round the bookshelf.

"It's that guy from your dad's band," Milo whispered.

Lucy's stomach did jumping jacks. *Scruffy Steve.* He was one of them. Why was he here? It couldn't be a coincidence. *Pretenders of a feather flock together.*

"Heya, Kenzo." Steve removed his soggy raincoat and hung it by the door. "You're looking as grim as the storm out there."

"I've seen brighter days, as have we all," replied Kenzo. He set the vase on the tarot table and gave the flowers a fluff. "But the skies will soon clear, if all goes according to plan."

Plan? What plan? Is this Kenzo dude one of them too?

"Has anyone else arrived for the meeting?" asked Steve. "I was told there would be cookies." He rubbed his belly.

"You're the first to arrive, my friend," said Kenzo. "Though there are a couple of customers lurking about."

Steve stood on his toes and peered across the room. "Is that purple hair I see?" He ambled over. "Lucy Goosie!"

He patted her on the back so hard she dropped her notebook to the floor with a FTONK. It flopped open to a page filled with scribbled names and hand-drawn pictures of the Pretenders in their various forms.

Criminy peatmoss! Lucy quickly kicked the

book behind her.

"H-hi, Steve," she stammered. "What are you doing here?"

"Little a' this, little a' that." Steve side-stepped the question. "Hey!" He pointed a couple of finger guns. "If it isn't Milo Fisher, the Kayak Kid."

"Hi, Mr Kozlowski." Milo stooped to pick up Lucy's notebook.

"No!" Lucy smacked the book out of his hands.

Milo scowled. "What's the matter with you?" He picked it up. The book lay open in his hands.

Crud! Crudcrudcrudcrud... "Please don't read that," she urged.

"I wasn't planning to." Milo shot her a scathing look.

"Are you guys here for the secret meeting?" Steve scratched his scraggly beard. "Seems a bit premature..."

Secret meeting? "Uh, we were just here to, to..." Lucy searched for a lie, any lie...

The chimes on the door jingled once more.

"Anybody home?" called a gruff female voice. "I wasn't sure what to bake, so I've brought gingerbread people of various persuasions." The Other Mrs Stricks set her picnic basket on the table next to the black roses. "Sladan?" she said, spotting Lucy. "What's she doing here? And why has she brought the boy?"

Lucy gulped. The place was filling up with Pretenders, all meeting here for some unknown purpose. She was starting to feel like she and Milo had accidentally stumbled into a beehive.

Mrs Stricks came into view, shaking off her umbrella. "Lucy?" She glared at Steve. "Did you tell her about this?"

"I thought you two invited her."

"And why would we do that?" said Mrs Stricks.

"I dunno." Steve scratched his head. "Nobody told me what the plan was."

"Shhhh!" hissed the Other Mrs Stricks. "Not in front of the boy!"

"We were just leaving," Lucy cut in.

She turned to Milo, whose eyes were glued to her open notebook. He looked green.

With a yelp Lucy snatched the book from his hands. "I told you not to read that!"

Milo took one look around the place, clocked the faces in the room, then bolted towards the door, knocking over the dreamcatcher stand on the way out.

"Be careful," the Other Mrs Stricks warned. "You wouldn't want to bring the whole place down, would you?"

Milo slammed the door behind him with a jangle. Lucy hurried after him.

Mrs Stricks looked concerned. "Lucita," she said. "What's the matter with Milo?"

"Oh, nothing." Lucy slid past the older ladies as politely as she could. "He's just, uh, allergic to sage."

"I told you we should hold the meeting at our house," said the Other Mrs Stricks as Lucy scurried past.

"And I suppose *you'd* have done the dishes,

dear?" Mrs Stricks scoffed.

Lucy quickly exited the store. Outside, the rain was falling harder than ever and the road was beginning to flood, the storm drains clogged with autumn leaves. Lucy splashed across the street, her glasses smeared with water. Milo was hunched over by the lamp post, struggling to unlock his bike.

"Fish," Lucy called.

The bike came unlatched and Milo hopped on. Lucy grabbed the handlebars.

"Where are you going?" she asked.

"What are those people?" Milo demanded.

Lucy was standing in the gutter, ankle-deep in water. She hesitated. "What do you mean? They're my neighbours."

"Stop lying." Milo wiped his wet nose with his sleeve. "I was right, wasn't I? There *are* more shapeshifters like Thingus, and they look just like us."

Lucy stared at the water flowing over her boots. "I wanted to tell you," she said. "But I couldn't. You have to understand—"

"I don't have to understand anything," said Milo. "You lied to me. Again. After I told you everything." He velcroed the front flap of his hood over his chin. "I stole from my father because you asked me to. I shared Thingus with you. You had a million chances to tell me the truth, and you lied."

"It's complicated," Lucy insisted. "I had to lie to protect them."

"Protect them?" Milo laughed. "From what?"

"From Nu Co.," said Lucy. "From your dad!"

"Why is everyone so fixated on my father?" Milo shouted. "I wouldn't have told him, anyway! You could have trusted me."

"You wouldn't talk to me!"

"Yeah," sniffed Milo. "For good reason." He pulled his bike out of her grip.

"Fish, wait," said Lucy.

He stopped and glared at her. Lucy tried to think of something to say, but she was at a loss.

"We're done, Lucita. Goodbye." Milo took

off, splashing her as he went.

"How am I supposed to get home?" Lucy called.

"Figure it out for yourself," said Milo, disappearing round the bend.

Lucy kicked the puddle at her feet. Everything was ruined, once again.

"Are you okay, little one?" said a voice from across the street.

Lucy turned to look. A woman was walking her bicycle in front of The Woo Woo Store. Curly red hair poked out from under her hood.

Marietta Corbin. Lucy shook her head. The hot tears on her cheeks mixed with the cold rain.

"Would you like to come inside?" Marietta asked, gesturing towards her shop. Her teal rain poncho fanned out like the wing of a peacock.

Lucy stifled a sob. She shook her head again.

Ms Corbin waded across the road with her bicycle. "Feeling in over your head?" she asked gently.

Unable to contain her feelings any longer,

Lucy began to cry in earnest.

"Here." Ms Corbin rolled the bike towards her. "Why don't you borrow this and get yourself someplace dry?"

Lucy took the handlebars with surprise. "But what about you?"

Marietta tilted her head skywards, letting the rain fall on her face. "Just bring it back tomorrow," she smiled. "I have other ways of getting where I'm going." She patted the bike and wandered into her store.

Lucy stood at the side of the road, unsure what to do about the multifaceted mess her life had become. *So much for the Truth*. Crestfallen, she hopped on Marietta's bike and started riding, headed anywhere but home.

CHAPTER 19

Crodbarres

Milo pedalled through the rain, alone once again. The situation was clearly worse than he'd imagined. A single shapeshifter in Black Hole Lake was one thing, but, according to Lucy's notes, half a dozen of the town's residents were part of some kind of invading supernatural force. How could she have lied to him again, after everything they'd experienced together? Enough was enough. It was time to tell his father what he knew.

Mr Fisher had been right, after all. About Lucy. About Sticky Pines. Who knows? Maybe he was right about boarding school in Kansas not being awful, too, which Milo was going to volunteer for as soon as he got home. But, first things first, he had to say goodbye to Thingus. It wasn't the poor creature's fault that he was a member of a potentially dangerous inhuman race. Milo didn't want to think about how much he was going to miss him.

Black Hole Lake was especially steamy this stormy November day. Fortunately, Milo was warm and dry inside his monsoon-grade rain gear. He hid his bike behind the usual bushes, pulled his kayak out from under the decrepit dock and hopped in.

The wind picked up as Milo paddled towards the Siren's Lair, rain hammering the lake's surface like fistfuls of gravel. It was late afternoon, but the sky was so darkened by heavy clouds it seemed night had fallen early.

"PHEW-EEEE OOO," Milo whistled. He hoped Thingus could hear him over the din. He slapped his oar on the surface. *Come on, buddy. One last time, please.*

Miraculously, Milo heard a bubbly response below: "PHBEEWWW-BEEEEEEE-BWOOOO." A moment later, a pair of small leathery hands emerged from the lake and clung to the front of the boat. Thingus, in the form of a river otter, climbed aboard, his cat-like teeth showing through a wide grin.

"Hey, pal," said Milo. "I like your new shape."

Thingus scampered down the length of the kayak and leapt into Milo's arms.

Milo hugged the otter close. "It's good to see you, too." The furry being wrapped itself round Milo's neck and chittered in his ear. "Come on, let's get out of the rain."

Thingus scurried to the tip of the kayak and stood on his hind legs like a sailor searching for land.

When they reached the island, Milo pulled the boat on to the shore and followed Thingus under the shelter of some trees just off the shallow beach. The rain pattered the evergreen branches and everything smelled like mud. Milo pulled back his yellow rain hood. *Oof. This is going to be hard.*

"Thingus," he began. *Goodbye, my friend. I have to go away, now. C'mon, just say it.* "I, um..."

The otter spun round in a circle, then stood up and clapped his webbed hands. He held them out like a duck-fingered orphan, hope radiating from his soft brown eyes.

"I'm sorry, pal. I don't have any candy."

Not one to take "no" for an answer, Thingus quivered, slimed and grew until he was as tall as Milo's waist. He scampered in a circle, showing off his new size, as if to say, "Look, I did a trick! Now give me some candy."

"You're amazing, you know that?" said Milo, his voice catching in his throat.

The otter took a two-footed step forward, but tripped on his thick tail. Milo caught him before he landed in the mud.

"Nice try," Milo chuckled, "but your legs are too short." He set the creature back on his feet.

Thingus gazed up at him and held out his hands again.

Milo looked away. "I have to tell you something," he said, his tone serious. "I'm really sorry, but I have to go away. Probably forever."

Thingus's smile faltered. He seemed confused. Milo felt a blow to his heart.

"I just... I can't live here any more." Milo punched a tree trunk, skinning his knuckles. "This whole town is crazy. Sticky Pines *makes* people crazy. There's no one I can trust. No one I can talk to. I have to leave. Now." He turned to go back to the shore, but Thingus wrapped his arms round Milo's leg.

Milo scratched the furry creature between the ears. "I'm sorry, little guy. It's not your fault. It's everyone else. It's Lucy. And my f-father." He slumped to the ground and buried his face between his knees, trying to keep the tears from spilling.

A breeze ruffled the hair on the back of his neck, and Milo felt a hand on his shoulder. *Huh?*

He raised his head and found himself staring into a pair of blue eyes very like his own. *What the– Who?*

Smiling down at him sympathetically, stooping under the low branches, was a boy about his age. Though the humanoid child's lips and brown skin tone mirrored Lucy's, the rest of his facial features resembled Milo's. His hair, though, was unique: thick, shaggy indigo curls falling down to his jawline. The kid appeared to be wearing yellow rain gear like Milo's, but his "clothes" had no fasteners, wrinkles or any other myriad details of Milo's own attire. The creature must have grown the clothing, like he'd grown hair and feathers before.

"Thingus?" Milo gasped.

The new kid grinned, a gap between his front teeth, like Lucy's.

"Since when did you learn to do *this*?"

Thingus held out his perfect human hand, and with a graceful strength, helped Milo to standing.

"Crodbarres," said Thingus. His otherworldly voice was a touch deeper than Milo's and vibrated like he was speaking through a spinning fan.

Son of a stockbroker. "Do you mean, 'crudberries'?" asked Milo.

The newly verbal being laughed.

His first word was "crudberries". Lucy would be so proud.

"Thingus," said Milo. "What are you?"

Thingus scrunched his nose and worked his jaw, still feeling out his new features. "Crodbarres," he said again.

A juddering, chopping sound interrupted Milo's thoughts. *What is that?*

Clearly unused to this new form, Thingus dropped down and crawled on his hands and knees towards the beach, spider-quick.

"Wait," said Milo, wriggling through the trees in pursuit.

On the shallow shore, Milo threw his hands over his ears to block out the deafening racket. Waves churned at the waterline as the wind gusted and swirled, hurling up rainwater and dead leaves that stung Milo's eyes. The wet stones glinted under the glare of a blindingly bright light. It wasn't the sun; the rain was falling as thickly as ever.

Thingus stood on the beach, squinting skywards.

A small projectile whizzed through the air past the freshly formed child's head. Startled, Thingus screamed like a banshee.

Milo turned to see a tranquilliser dart sticking out of the mud behind them. He whipped back round, finally realising what he was seeing. It was a helicopter. *My father has found us.*

Milo yanked Thingus back towards the shelter of the trees.

THWAP!

A dart hit Thingus in the leg.

"No!" yelled Milo.

Thingus fell to the ground, wailing in confusion. The young humanoid's skin began to shimmer and, with more effort than usual, he transformed back into a stag, bucking and thrashing at the sky.

Milo ran out into the open, waving his arms at the helicopter. "Stop!" he shouted. "Please!"

The stag reared up at its attackers. Then he inhaled deeply and started to grow.

"Thingus, don't," Milo begged. "You can't fight a helicopter."

But the creature continued to expand until he was the size of a station wagon. Raising up on his hind legs, he released an angry bellow at the chopper.

SCHLUPPK! A massive wad of steaming pink goo shot from a cannon mounted on the side of the helicopter, hitting Thingus square in the chest and splattering across the deer's neck and legs. Thingus swayed, disoriented. SCHLUPPK! Another wad smashed into the creature's torso. Jerking and keening like the wild animal he'd become, Thingus desperately tried to shake off the unknown substance without success. Stumbling about, he shimmered, trying to shift his shape, but he was now unable to change form.

Milo inhaled a nauseating scent, both acrid and sweet. *Nucralose*. This is what his father had been working on all this time. He'd re-engineered the tree sap once again, targeting the Pretenders. Somehow, he'd found a way to prevent them from using their shapeshifting powers. *How long has Dad known about them?* Milo now realised what his father had meant when he said he'd found a way to solve the "Sticky Pines problem".

Milo waved his arms at the helicopter, hollering for it to back off, but as he did so Thingus was hit with another tranquilliser dart, this time directly in the neck. The giant stag's muscles seized up and he fell heavily on to the rocky beach.

"Thingus!" Milo cried.

The helicopter hovered over the shore, black ropes dropping down from its side.

Unsure what to do, Milo grabbed the mighty deer by its goo-splattered forelimbs and tried to drag him into the trees. It was no use; the creature was far too heavy.

"Step away from the target," a megaphoned voice barked from the helicopter.

Four muscular figures in black tactical gear slid down the dangling ropes. One of them, a square-jawed man wearing an infrared visor and helmet, tackled Milo and pulled him into the bushes. He propped the boy up on a fallen log while the other security professionals strapped Thingus to an oversized stretcher.

"Stay here," the man ordered Milo. He spoke into a device on his wrist. "Eaglet is disentangled. Rogue Deviant is neutralised."

The sturdy squaddie ran back to join his compatriots. Milo watched in horror as the men threw a set of thick nylon straps round Thingus.

Milo mentally kicked himself. How could he be so reckless? Of course his father had tracked him to the island. He must have known about his visits to Thingus for days, if not longer. Milo had tried to be so careful, to inspect his shoes, to only wear clothing he had stored in his locker at school. Sure, he'd only wiped his phone's memory the one time, but there was never any reception in Sticky Pines, so he didn't think– *Blue blazers.* Milo opened his mobile. Sure enough, an app he'd never noticed before was tracking his location. *Stupid, stupid, stupid...*

He ran towards the lake and – "NYAH!" – threw the device into the choppy water with all his might.

"Hey, kid," yelled the squaddie. He was busily fastening a harness around Thingus. "Get back here!"

But Milo didn't stop. He ran straight into the water and jumped into his kayak, casting off on to the lake. The men didn't pursue him: they were too busy securing the sizable stag. They hoisted him into the air, teetering precariously as he was pulled up beneath the helicopter. The security goons jumped on to the remaining ropes, and were themselves pulled up into the helicopter's cabin in turn. The chopper dipped its nose and sped off towards the Nu Co. complex.

What do I do, what do I do, what do I do? Milo paddled frantically, the rain pounding on his hood synching with the beat of his heart.

CHAPTER 20

Cliff's Edge

The fire crackled behind Lucy's damp parka, which was slung over the back of a chair by the Arkhipovs' brick fireplace. Seated cross-legged on the floral couch, Lucy thrashed Tex's shirtless avatar with her electrified green beast. She picked up Tex's beefcake, did a backflip and slammed him across the video game screen, the words "KO" appearing in dripping red letters. *Boo ya.*

"If I did not know any better," said Tex, "I might think you had some aggression to work out."

"I told you," said Lucy, "I don't wanna talk

about it." She took a swig of hot chocolate. Anna Arkhipov had made a large batch when Lucy showed up at the door looking like something Errol had pulled out of a bog.

"Would you like more pretzels, Lucy dear?" Tex's mother called from the kitchen.

Lucy inspected the empty party bowl. "Yes, please, Mrs Arkhipov!"

"And we will also take the leftover Halloween candy," called Tex.

Anna poked her head around the door frame. "I told you, Alexei, only three pieces per day."

Tex squeezed Lucy's cheeks until she resembled a chipmunk. "But look at this sad girl. She needs sugar."

Sighing, Anna disappeared and returned with a bowl of candy. "Do not tell Toli." She gestured upstairs towards her youngest son's bedroom.

"Please." Tex grabbed a bite-sized chocolate bar. "His music can be heard a block away. He has no idea we are even here."

Anna waltzed back into the kitchen, humming

"Looking for Freedom" by David Hasselhoff.

Tex stretched his thumbs. "Time for a new game." He picked out another cartridge and inserted it into the console.

Lucy pouted.

"Okay, seriously, what is up?" Tex plopped on to the couch beside her. "Is it Feesh?

Lucy grunted. "I don't wanna talk about that dingus."

"Aha. And why is he a dingus this time?"

The pair chose their cars and characters.

"The truth is," said Lucy, "Fish and I have a fundamental incompatibility in the way we assimilate an ever-shifting reality."

"That sounds serious."

"Let's go!" announced the game.

Tex and Lucy shimmied on the couch, thumbs flailing as they tried to beat each other to the finish line.

"But I thought –" Tex whooped as his car dodged the oil slick Lucy shot at him – "you guys were star-crossed besties."

Lucy's car hit a ramp and nearly careened off the edge of the rainbow-coloured road. "I think we're just crossed." She hammered the A button, activating the turbo boost. "And besides," she said, slamming Tex's vehicle into a wall, "*you're* my bestie."

"Eat this!" Tex shot a jet of fire in Lucy's skeletal avatar's face, leaving her to languish in a cloud of smoke as he crossed the finish line. *This guy knows the meaning of true friendship.*

KNOCK, KNOCK, KNOCK, KNOCK, KNOCK!

Someone pounded insistently on the front door.

"Alexei," yelled his mother. "My hands are soapy, will you get that?"

Tex hit pause and answered the door.

A bedraggled boy wearing what looked like a hazmat suit stood on the front porch, dripping with sweat and rain. His bike lay haphazardly at the foot of the porch.

"Is Lucy here?" Milo panted.

"Speak of the devil." Tex glanced over his shoulder.

What on the round blue Earth is HE doing here? Lucy mouthed the word "NO" to Tex.

"Sorry," said Tex. "She says she is not here."

Milo shivered in the cold.

"But it is wet as an octopus disco out there," said Tex. "Come on inside."

"Sorry," said Milo, "there's no time. Can you tell her this is really important?"

Curiosity getting the best of her, Lucy came to the door. "What?" she asked flatly.

"I need your help," said Milo.

"How did you know I was here?"

"You weren't at your house. I figured this is the next place you'd be." Milo spoke rapidly. "Listen, you have to come with me. Please."

"Come with you? You said you didn't trust me. And, you know what, I'm not sure I trust *you*—"

Milo grabbed her by the shoulders. "It's Thingus."

Lucy's face fell. "What happened?"

"What's Thingus?" said Tex, sifting through the candy bowl.

"It was my dad's security team," said Milo, his voice cracking. "They showed up in a helicopter with all this gunk and gadgets. Lucy, they took Thingus."

"They took Thingus!" she exclaimed.

"What is THINGUS?" Tex asked again.

Lucy grabbed her damp parka, knocking over the chair it was draped over. "Thanks for the eats, Mrs Arkhipov!" she yelled as she shoved her rain boots on and ran out the door after Milo.

"Thingus schmingus," Tex grumbled.

He turned round just in time to see Toli snatch the candy bowl from the coffee table and run upstairs.

"Come back with that, you fart dragon!" Tex shouted, slamming the front door behind him.

Lucy struggled to keep up with Milo as he raced ahead on the slick roadway.

"I don't understand," she huffed. "How did

they catch him? Why didn't he transform into a small creature and hide?"

"They surprised us," Milo yelled over his shoulder. "Then they disabled Thingus with this horrible pink goo."

Lucy gasped. *The pink smoke at the geodesic dome. That's what all the sap is for. Nu Co. is making a weapon against the Pretenders!*

They flew round a bend. Lucy skidded on a patch of leaves, but she righted her bike before she slid into the trees. Milo hardly seemed to notice.

"What do you think they're going to do to Thingus?" asked Milo. His face was lit by the ghostly red glow of his bike light, his brow tight with worry.

Lucy tried to push the word "dissect" to the back of her mind. "I really don't know."

"I just thought..." Milo trailed off. "You seem to know all there is to know about everything that's happening around here."

"You have no idea how much I wish that was

true," Lucy responded.

When they reached the top of Nu Co.'s driveway, the security gate was locked. Though the parking lot had a scattering of cars in it, the factory appeared to be shuttered and empty.

Lucy stuck her fingers through the chain-link fence. "I bet they took Thingus to the secret lab."

"Secret lab?" said Milo.

"There's a hidden entrance in the middle of the orchard," said Lucy. "That's where they're taking all the sap."

"Take me there," said Milo.

Lucy scaled the chain-link fence, Milo scrambling after her.

They raced down the driveway, their breath fogging in the cold night air, the cascading sheets of rain muffling their footsteps. Without warning Milo tackled Lucy from behind and yanked her into the foliage at the side of the road.

"Hey!" she yelped.

He silenced her with a finger to her lips, then pointed up. A drone with a sweeping spotlight flew across the driveway ahead of them.

Their rescue mission had nearly ended as soon as it had begun. They'd have to be careful from here on out. *Which is going to be difficult, considering Milo's dressed like Big Bird.*

"About your clothes..." said Lucy.

Without hesitation Milo stripped off his raincoat and trousers, revealing a pair of khakis and a black fleece jacket. Although he'd be soaked in seconds, he was much less likely to be seen. Lucy handed him her purple scarf and he wrapped it around his head like a balaclava.

Slipping in and out of the trees, they made their way towards the centre of the orchard. Milo scanned the skies, pulling Lucy this way or that to avoid detection. At last, they reached the thick grove of sticky pines surrounding the geodesic dome.

Milo and Lucy ducked through the undergrowth to the edge of the grove, then hid behind a heavy indigo tree branch. The white dome glowed in the darkness, illuminated by dim lights. Today, the smoke emanating from the pipe on the top of the futuristic building was a pale blue colour, rather than pink.

Guess they're working on some new experimental monstrosity.

A stocky man stood watch on the grated porch, an earpiece snaking along his soft chin. *Mr Murl.* Of course Fisher's most heinous henchman was guarding the entrance. Instead of a suit and tie, he wore a set of black military-style tactical gear. *What's he up to?*

"Are you sure this is the right place?" Milo whispered. "It's not nearly big enough to house a secret lab."

"It's in there," said Lucy. "Trust me."

"How do we get past Murl?" Milo lamented. "They're probably experimenting on Thingus as we speak."

CRACKKKKK! A bolt of lightning struck the orchard about thirty metres north. Lucy and Milo jumped in alarm.

"What was that?" Unnerved, Murl stalked off

his post towards the treeline. "You sure that's just normal lightning?" He paused, listening to someone on his earpiece. "Send a drone," he barked, then turned back towards the dome.

Dratsicle sticks.

Milo's teeth chattered. How long could they wait out here before he got hypothermia?

Come on. Think, Lucita! There's gotta be a way past this slugmunch.

MYYOOOOOOOOOOOOOWWWWWWWWWWWNNGGRRRRR.

A high-pitched wail, like the cry of a demonic baby, rang out from the area where the lightning had struck.

"Is that a cat?" Murl said to whoever was on the other end of the line.

MWWWOOOOOWOWWWWWWWWWWRRRRR! The yowl sounded again, louder and more insistent.

"Cats make that noise?" whispered Milo.

"It's called caterwauling," said Lucy. "They do it when they're fighting over territory and stuff. They don't normally come out in the rain, though." She remembered the local weatherman morphing into a feline just the other day. "I'll bet it's not really a cat, though."

"You think it's a Pretender?"

Lucy nodded, feeling a tremendous rush of relief at finally being able to speak about such things with her friend. "Maybe they're coming for Thingus."

Milo's expression looked somewhere between heartened and horrified.

I hope the Pretenders are *here. We could use all the help we can get.*

"I'm telling you," Murl snarled, "that ain't no normal cat." He pulled a high-tech-looking tranquilliser gun from its holster and took off into the trees.

"Let's go," said Lucy.

Quickly, the kids raced over to the entrance to the geodesic structure. Milo yanked on the heavy door, but it wouldn't budge.

Lucy pointed to the number pad on the wall.

"You need a code to get in."

"A code?" Milo ripped the scarf off his head and threw it on the ground. "What are we supposed to do now?"

"Relax, Fish."

"Relax? Thingus is in danger and there's nothing we can do and you want me to relax? If we don't—"

"I've got the code right here." Lucy waved her unicorn notebook in front of his face.

Milo stopped pacing. "You do?" He threw his arms round her. "You're a superhero."

Blushing, Lucy punched the numbers into the keypad. It beeped, and with a CLICK the heavy door opened.

"I'll never doubt you again," said Milo, hustling through the doorway.

"I want that in writing." Lucy snatched up her scarf and slipped inside, bracing herself for Mr Fisher's latest house of horrors.

CHAPTER 21

Subterranean Science

Milo burst into the small white dome and gasped at what resembled the aftermath of a bubblegum explosion: the smooth white floor and curved geodesic walls were spattered with streaks of pink goo. Clearly, Thingus had been here, and he'd struggled mightily against his captors.

The dome wasn't a laboratory, but rather an entrance chamber containing nothing but a set of three silver elevator doors. The call buttons pointed in only one direction: down.

"I guess the secret lab is more of an underground lair," said Lucy.

"Don't call my dad's lab a lair."

They headed into the middle elevator, which was also covered in smears of pink goo. *Thingus must be so frightened,* worried Milo. If only his father knew that the shapeshifter wasn't a monster, none of this would be happening. *I wonder if Dad's scared, too.* Then he remembered seeing photos of his father out lion hunting in Mozambique. He hadn't seemed scared then.

The buttons on the elevator wall indicated there were three floors below ground: "minus one", "minus two" and "minus three". Milo pushed "minus one", and the elevator began to whirr. *We're coming for you, Thingus.*

"What do we do if they catch us?" asked Lucy.

"We could tell the truth. Maybe my dad would let Thingus go?"

"As much as I'd like to believe that, do you really think it would work?"

Milo didn't respond. They both knew the answer.

The elevator doors opened with a DUNG, revealing a dank hall with walls composed of multicoloured stones arranged in swirling patterns.

"This is like the tunnel under the factory," whispered Lucy. "Where we found the missing people."

They were rather far from the factory now, but Milo remembered that the tunnel beneath it had seemed to stretch on and on. Here, the old corridor had been modernised. The craggy ceiling had been outfitted with stark fluorescent lights, and the walls with sturdy silver hatch doors.

Cautiously, Milo and Lucy crept along the cobblestone floor. They peeked through a small window in the first door on the left and spied a white-walled room filled with scientific equipment. Several people in lab coats worked diligently inside, fiddling with microscopes, test tubes and Bunsen burners.

A woman in a hairnet and goggles placed a beaker containing a dark, syrupy substance over one of the burners. She added a yellow liquid to the beaker with an eyedropper. The substance bubbled and emitted a plume of sky-blue smoke.

"What do you think they're making in there?" whispered Lucy.

Just then, a pair of male scientists strolled from the back of the room towards the door.

Milo ducked below the window, pulling Lucy down with him. "Someone's coming."

They raced across the hall into an unused presentation room containing worktables and filing cabinets.

Now they could hear the men's voices in the hallway: "The sap's chemical structure is incredibly malleable," said the first voice. "I've never seen anything like it."

"And it's so abundant," said the second. "It's coming from the trees, but surely it can't all be coming FROM the trees."

The men's footsteps clacked across the stone corridor.

"They're headed in here," whispered Lucy. "Hide!"

They scurried under a table at the back of the room. A moment later, the men entered.

"It's remarkable, isn't it?" said the first man, the elder of the two. He had close-cropped white hair and sun-speckled skin. "There are still so many undiscovered treasures in the unkempt backwaters of this great nation." He lowered himself stiffly into an ergonomic chair.

Lucy's face contorted into a sneer. "That's Doctor VINK," she mouthed, then mimed sticking her finger down her throat.

According to Milo's father, Vink was an expert in psychobiology, neurobotany and golf. Milo had met him a few times before. The last time had been under the factory, where the doctor had been performing experiments on the missing people.

"I still can't wrap my head round the potential value of these resources," said the younger man, whom Milo didn't recognise. He was stout and bespectacled, with an impeccably groomed beard. Rifling through a drawer, he chose a file and handed it to Vink. "Fisher was right. This sap is miraculous. I've never seen anything like it."

Doctor Vink examined the file. "But before these resources can be fully exploited, Doctor Bell, the local threat must be eliminated."

"Speaking of which," said Bell, "have the tests begun on our new guest downstairs?"

Lucy gripped Milo's wrist.

They're talking about Thingus. Milo's jaw clenched. *He's not on this floor.*

Vink smirked. "The deviant organism is contained for now. Feisty things, these Pretenders."

Lucy dug her nails into Milo's skin. "Ouch," he hissed.

Bell turned. "Did you hear something?"

A startled scream echoed down the hallway.

Vink stood up so fast both he and his chair nearly toppled over.

A small black-and-white animal scrabbled past their door and down the hallway, chased by a gaggle of people in white coats.

"Was that a cat?" asked Vink.

"We're not lab-testing felines, are we?" said Doctor Bell.

Grumbling, the men hurried out into the hallway and followed the group to the right.

"Let's go," said Milo.

The pair raced out of the room in the opposite direction and hurtled into the elevator. Panting, Lucy's hand hovered over the buttons. "Which floor?"

"I don't know," said Milo. "They just said he was downstairs."

Lucy shrugged and pressed the button for the bottom level, "minus three". The elevator kicked into action, continuing its downwards journey for what seemed like an age. Milo shifted anxiously. *Come on, come on, come on.* How far underground were they going?

The bell dinged and the elevator doors opened. A hot gust of sulphuric air smacked their faces. Guardedly, they exited the compartment into a vast cave of yellow stone illuminated by large portable spotlights. Its ceiling dripped with glittering stalactites.

"What is this place?" said Milo.

He and Lucy ventured into the strange cavern. They appeared to be alone, though a row of hard hats and heavy-duty boots lay on a bench near the elevators.

The cave's rocky walls, easily three storeys tall, were decorated from top to bottom with countless ancient-looking carvings: hieroglyphic symbols, images of plants and trees, stellar constellations, and an array of animals from a lowly banana slug to a rhinoceros to a spindly human figure holding a spear. Intermingled with the images were depictions of bizarre creatures with jumbled features. Some had animal bodies with human heads. Some had the reverse arrangement. Milo recognised some of the uncanny hybrids from the mythological creatures described in his cryptozoology book.

"It's like the Siren Stone," murmured Lucy.

"But MEGA." She spun round to take in the immensity of the find.

"Do you think the Pretenders made all this?" he asked. There was so much to see it was almost overwhelming. "How long have they been here?"

"Over a hundred years, for sure," said Lucy. "The Other Mrs Stricks is at least that old."

"Are you serious?" said Milo, alarmed. "How is that possible?"

"I dunno. How is any of this possible?" Lucy adjusted her glasses and peered, wide-eyed, at a six-foot carving of a man with the head of a buffalo and flames where his eyes should have been. "That's exactly what I want to find out."

Milo approached a knobbly stone column covered in carvings of hand, paw and claw prints. He traced one of the prints with a finger. *Were any of these made by Thingus?* He tried to count them all, but there were too many. "How many Pretenders *are* there?"

"Nine that I know of, including Thingus."

"But this cave is insane," said Milo, feeling

overwhelmed. "Either the Pretenders are way older than a hundred—"

"Or there are more of them than we think there are," said Lucy, eagerly taking down a note.

"Doesn't any of this worry you?"

"They've been my neighbours my whole life, Fish. Why would they worry me?"

"Because there's so much about them that we don't know."

"What worries me," said Lucy, "is never finding out the Truth about any of this. If there's one certainty in the universe, it's that there's TONS of things out there that we don't know about. There's so much that we'll never even begin to imagine with our puny little brains! But it's definitely out there, existing, whether we like it or not. What's the point in being afraid of stuff just because you don't understand it?"

"But what if the Pretenders are, like, evil?"

"Do you know of any species on the planet that's all good or all evil?" Lucy retorted. "Is Thingus evil?"

"This is giving me a headache," said Milo. He wrenched his attention away from the mysterious discovery. "Thingus isn't here. We need to go find him."

"I know," Lucy whimpered. "But can you at least take some pictures of this place first? We may never get a chance to come back."

"Good idea." Milo patted his back pocket, then winced as he remembered. "Except my phone is at the bottom of Black Hole Lake."

Lucy kicked a stalagmite. "Why do I never have access to a functioning camera at times like this?" She hastily sketched some of the glyphs in her notebook as Milo pulled her into the elevator.

He pressed the button to go one floor up, to "minus two". By the process of elimination Thingus must surely be there. Milo's stomach churned in anticipation. The doors opened.

The raucous din of human activity assaulted their senses. Milo and Lucy slammed their backs against the side wall of the elevator to hide from sight. Footsteps, voices and the ratchets and bangs of heavy machinery echoed around the hall.

"Did anyone see us?" whispered Lucy.

"If they did, I think we'd know." Milo stuck his head though the open elevator door.

The hallway on this floor was wider than the first, with smooth cement walls and strip lighting. The clanking noises of industry were emanating from a series of large rooms on the left side of the corridor. Lucy and Milo slipped out into the hall.

"So," Milo whispered, "what's the plan to rescue Thingus?"

"There's a plan?"

"No. That's the problem." They peeked through a window in the first door, upon which the words "Aerial Projectile Defence" had been painted in red letters.

Inside the room, several men and women in lab coats sat at a row of computers situated behind a thick panel of plexiglass. Beyond it, a small cannon-like apparatus sat twenty metres away from a wall covered in bullseyes. One of the scientists punched a series of commands into his computer, and, with a BANG, the cannon shot a glob of raw black sap, which hit one of the targets with a STHPLUNK. All the scientists in the room cheered.

Is this supposed to be a serious workplace?

Lucy pulled Milo's elbow and led him down the corridor to the next test chamber. There, two scientists clad in heavily padded safety gear were dousing a crash-test dummy with buckets of sticky black sap. When the figure was covered from head to toe, they retreated to the sides of the room. A third scientist, wearing a soot-stained backpack made of metal canisters, stepped out into the centre of the chamber and shot a forceful jet of flame at the glazed mannequin: SHGKKKKXXXRRGHH!

"The employees at Nu Co. are allowed to use FLAMETHROWERS?" whispered Lucy.

"It certainly beats working in a cubicle," said Milo.

He ducked down and urged Lucy along to the next room, where the door was ajar. Finger to his lips, he tiptoed to the edge of the door frame.

The right side of this laboratory housed dozens of stacked cages containing white mice. Each cage was mounted with a dispenser filled with unnaturally coloured food pellets: pink, gold and blue. On the left side of the room, in a pair of much larger cages, two chimpanzees jumped and hooted in agitation. A scientist with mussed hair and red sneakers crouched by the cage, his back to Milo. He repeatedly attempted to feed one of the chimps a banana dripping with golden syrup that looked like Nucralose. The angry ape kept slapping the banana away.

"All right, Bobo, we tried the easy way," said the man. "Colleen!"

A statuesque ponytailed woman emerged from behind the mouse cages carrying a long tube with a rubber bag attached to one end.

Lucy clenched her fists, surely wanting to rush in and break open all the cage doors.

Without warning Milo felt something ruffle the back of his hair. Swatting at the air in confusion, he looked up to see a magpie flying low over his head and into the animal-testing room, where it perched on the chimps' cage, startling the scientists.

"Are they keeping birds in the lab down the hall?" said the man, perplexed.

A second magpie, smaller than the first, swooped in and fluttered around his head, squawking like a demon.

"I'll get the net, Fred," said Colleen. She abruptly turned round and spotted Milo and Lucy in the open doorway. "Hey, there's a couple of kids out there!" she exclaimed.

"Run!" yelled Milo.

He and Lucy barrelled down the hall, frantically checking each room they passed for any sign of Thingus. Angry shouting reverberated around the corridor behind them.

RAAAAAAXXXXXAAGHH! The muffled

sound of a monstrous inhuman howl sounded further down the tunnel.

There he is!

Milo raced down the corridor at top speed, finally reaching a pair of swinging double doors, the source of the bellowing wail.

"I'm coming, Thingus!" cried Milo.

"Wait!" yelled Lucy. "We don't know what's in there!"

But there was no time left for hesitation. Heroically, Milo ploughed through the doors, Lucy at his heels.

CHAPTER 22

Substance Nu-791

The double doors swung shut behind Lucy as she slid to a halt next to Milo, her hiking boots screeching on the cement floor. They had entered a wide windowless room lined with buzzing and burbling experimental equipment. *This place is a mad scientist's wildest dream.*

At the far end of the chamber, Mr Fisher stood amongst half a dozen scientists and tactically suited security officers all staring in shock at the kids' sudden appearance. The group was crowded around the room's scientific centrepiece: a cylindrical glass tank as big as an elephant, bolted to the floor and sealed at the top with a metal cap. Inside, a jet-black tentacled being floated in effervescent liquid, its listless dolphin-sized body covered in dozens of clear tubes and colourful electrodes.

Lucy could sense the creature's anguish from where she stood. *What have they done to you, Thingus?*

Mr Fisher returned his son's panicked glare. "How did you get down here?" he demanded.

"Let him go," Milo pleaded.

Hearing the sound of Milo's voice, Thingus's yellow eyes flew open in his catfish face. He sloshed urgently against the glass, the bubbly water churning around him. Milo ran towards the tank, but his father blocked his way.

Stringy Dum and squat Dummer emerged from behind the vessel, marching in lockstep towards Milo and Lucy. Fisher raised his hand and the goons stopped, awaiting his signal.

Fisher bowed his head. "Milo, you can't possibly expect me to release this monster."

"He's not a monster," said Lucy. "Thingus is

awesome. And smarter than you, probably."

"He's my friend, Dad," said Milo. "Please."

"Don't be absurd," said Fisher. "This creature is far better off in a secure lab than out there, endangering the community."

"You're the one who's dangerous," Lucy shot back, "with your deranged tests and experiments."

One of the scientists stepped forward, a petite woman with a tight black bun, red cat-eye glasses gracing her angular face.

Lucy's lip curled. *Doctor Quittan.*

"If we can put the children back in their cribs now, Richard," said Quittan, "the work must continue." She was carrying a sizable syringe.

Quittan was the head of chemical research at Nu Co. Lucy had previously encountered her at the Par-T in Da Pines carnival (*ugh*), and again at the factory. She remembered the woman as being overly fascinated by horrific bodily transformations and not especially keen on unannounced guests. She and Doctor Vink were the leaders of Fisher's torturous endeavours, and had probably been voted "Most Likely to Commit War Crimes'" in their high-school yearbooks.

Turning on her stiletto heel, Quittan approached Thingus's prison tank and lifted a cover to reveal a panel at the side.

"Introducing Substance Nu-791." She drove the needle into the rubber injection site. A pale blue liquid travelled slowly through a thick intravenous tube and into Thingus's torso.

The sky-blue substance appeared to have the opposite effect of the pink goo. Thingus's body began to change uncontrollably: his eight limbs melted together into a snake-like, singular form, then split into two stork-like legs, which thickened and split once more to form four mammalian appendages. Simultaneously, his head and neck lengthened and then shrank, widened, then winnowed. The other scientists took notes as the creature thrashed and wailed.

"Stop it," Milo begged Quittan. "You're hurting him!"

Doctor Quittan shot Fisher a look of disgust, imploring him to silence the boy.

Fisher snapped his fingers for Dum and Dummer to advance.

Lucy and Milo ran in different directions. Their only hope was to break Thingus out of the oversized vessel before he was irreparably harmed.

Dummer, the shorter of the goons and faster than he looked, nabbed Lucy by the elbow and pinned her arms behind her back. Milo zagged away but Dum, with a sinister grin, caught him by the collar and held him fast.

Lucy struggled to free herself as Thingus's anguished body morphed again and again, until finally his spasms ceased. The poor creature now had the body of a small deer, the head of an exotic lizard, and giant albatross wings that floated limply in the water. Thingus's scaly forehead was pressed against the glass, his mouth open in a soundless cry for help.

"What are you doing to him?" said Milo, straining against Dum's grip.

"It was Richard's ingenious idea," said Quittan, nodding at Fisher. "We've been developing ways to use the deviant species' own biological morphology to incapacitate it."

"Huh?" said Lucy.

"We're stopping the creatures from transforming at will," said a younger ginger-haired scientist. "The pink stuff prevents the creature from changing shape, and the blue stuff causes it to change uncontrollably." He tapped his clipboard with his pen. "Pretty neat, huh?"

"That's horrible," Lucy growled.

"Oh, don't worry," the man insisted. "This creature doesn't feel pain the same way we do."

I'll bet that's what you dillweeds say about the chimps, too.

"Of course he does," said Milo. "Just look at him! He's in agony."

Fisher shook his head. "You don't know

anything about this creature."

"Do *you*?" said Milo.

"I know it's not like us." Fisher motioned to his flunkies.

Dummer dragged Lucy towards the entrance as she kicked his shins in protest. Dum marched Milo to a chair by the door and forced him to sit. Red-faced, the boy tried to stand, but he was pushed back down decisively.

Mr Fisher approached his son. "Milo," he said, "I've been trying to protect you by keeping you out of all this, but I see now that that was a mistake. I think it's time you learned the truth about Sticky Pines."

Milo exchanged a glance with Lucy, who was dangling indignantly under Dummer's stinky armpit.

Fisher bent down, his hands on his knees. "That creature over there is not alone," he said, gravely. "You may find this hard to believe, but some of the people in this town are not what they seem. Milo, they're not *human*."

"Yeah. We already know that," said Lucy, rolling her eyes.

"Dad, listen to me," said Milo. "Thingus isn't a threat to anyone. I've spent every day with him for the past few weeks. He's no different from me or Lucy. You can't just torture him. Please, Dad, let him go."

"These monsters are not our friends," said Fisher. "They've attacked my machines."

"They just wanna stop *you* from destroying *them,*" said Lucy. She tried to wriggle out of Dummer's grasp, but he twisted her arm until she doubled over in pain.

Ignoring her, Fisher focused on his son. "That creature over there is *more* than just a threat."

"What do you mean?" asked Milo.

"It's an opportunity." Fisher gestured to the prison tank with pride. "This species has abilities beyond what anyone thought biologically possible. What we learn from it could result in the birth of a new way of life for all mankind."

Here we go. Lucy had heard Fisher ramble

on like this before. He couched his ambition in romantic notions of progress and discovery, but she could see through it: the man just wanted to make money. *He may as well have dollar signs for eyes*. When she looked over to Milo, though, he seemed more confused than ever.

Thingus cried out as Quittan approached his tank with another syringe filled with the nasty blue substance.

Milo snapped out of his bewilderment. "Stop hurting him!" he yelled.

The lights flickered, then dimmed as an alarm began to blare. WOMP! WOMP! WOMP!

"What's this now?" muttered Fisher.

Dummer's grip on Lucy loosened.

She seized her chance and stomped on his foot, then twisted out of his reach. The flustered goon swiped at thin air, missing her by a hair.

Before Dummer could chase her, his attention was diverted by the sound of loud voices in the hallway and an odd banging that sounded like… *What is that, hoofbeats?* The security duo booked it out into the hall, panicked shouting filling the room as the doors swung closed behind them.

Lucy sprinted towards Thingus. The ginger-haired scientist scrambled out of her way as she leapt in the air and threw a flying kick at the tank, hitting it with a solid THONK, but failing to break the thick glass. She slid to the ground, her knee aching. *Cripesauce.*

Fumbling for her glasses, which had fallen on the floor, Lucy was confronted by a pair of pointy leopard-print shoes.

"Nice try," said Quittan, looking smug. "But the glass is fortified."

The ceiling sprinkler system activated and a second alarm began to blare.

Lucy slipped on her glasses. "Who says I'm done trying?"

"Scotty, seize the girl," Quittan commanded.

The red-haired scientist looked around as if unsure she was speaking to him. He half-heartedly reached for Lucy. Too fast to be caught, she darted round the tank, looking for another way to break the vessel.

Energised, Thingus squealed, flapping his albatross wings and twisting against the tubes embedded in his furry torso.

"Can somebody please get the girl away from the asset?" yelled Fisher, holding Milo in place.

CLONK! The lab doors swung inwards as Dum ran into the room, swatting at a magpie with iridescent teal wings that was pecking at his head.

Lucy recognised it as one of the birds that had invaded the animal-testing room. *That's not one of Nu Co.'s test subjects*, she realised, *that's a Pretender!*

"Get it off me! Get it off," yelled Dum.

A puddle of black gelatinous goo trickled under the still swinging doors, seeming to move of its own accord. It congealed and transformed into a second larger magpie with a black head and white chest. The magpie flapped its wings and darted up to the ceiling, then dive-bombed Quittan.

The doctor grabbed an IV stand and tried to bat the bird away.

Milo broke free from his father and ran to Lucy, clinging to her side.

"What's happening?" he said.

"I told you the Pretenders were coming to free Thingus!" she exclaimed.

PAKKKROSHH!

The double doors flew off their hinges as a massive tawny mountain goat with enormous curled horns rammed its way into the room. Head down, muscled legs pounding at full speed, the mighty ibex tilted at the glass prison.

SMASHK-K-KKSH!

The ibex hit the tank with tremendous force. The impact created a web of cracks that spread and crackled until the container shattered, foamy liquid cascading to the floor. Thingus clambered out of the broken vessel and wilted to the ground. Spluttering, he opened his albatross wings, which spanned at least three metres, then shook off the remaining tubes and electrodes from his body. Standing on shaky legs, he raised his reptilian head and howled like a coyote: "OWOOOOOOOOOOOOH!"

Milo threw his arms round Thingus's neck, while Lucy buried her face in his soggy feathers. The creature purred, nuzzling Milo's shoulder.

Meanwhile, the ibex Pretender cornered the team of cowering scientists. It bowed its horned head and pawed the floor, snorting.

Doctor Quittan shrieked and scurried out through the busted doorway and into the hall. Scotty and the last of the white coats hustled after her, the goat thundering close behind.

The smell of smoke wafted through the lab's open threshold. A fire had clearly broken out somewhere down the hall.

I did wonder whether using a flamethrower indoors was a good idea…

"We need to get above ground," Fisher called, poised at the doorway.

"I'm not leaving without Thingus," said Milo. He coughed as the smoke thickened.

"Fine." Fisher held out his hands, as if in surrender. "If it's the only way to get you to safety," he said, "you can bring that Thing to the surface."

Milo burst into a grin. "Thank you!"

Lucy led the way through the broken doors and into the hazy hallway, looking anxiously at Fisher as she passed. Thingus trotted after her, his hooves clacking as clumsily as a newborn calf, his oversized wings dragging on the ground. Milo followed close behind, while Fisher brought up the rear.

Her eyes stinging, Lucy spotted a trail of white mice racing out of the animal-testing room and towards the exit. She paused to check inside. The cages were open and empty, and the chimps were nowhere to be seen. *The Pretenders must have gotten them out!*

As they ran further down the hallway, flames flickered angrily inside the testing rooms they had previously passed. An explosion sent a hail of sparks surging from a door at their side.

Lucy screamed and fell back against the corridor wall.

"Keep moving!" Fisher bellowed, emerging from a thick cloud of smoke.

They ran until they reached the elevator. Lucy pressed the call button repeatedly.

"Not that way," Fisher croaked. He gestured to the end of the hall. "There."

Lucy raced through an open door to an emergency staircase. The last of Fisher's scientists were several flights up, sprinting towards the top. Smoke billowed upwards through the shaft, illuminated by flashing red emergency lights. The stairway seemed endless.

Thingus bumped into Lucy as he rushed fearfully through the door, Milo at his side. With no other possible route to safety, they galloped up flight after flight of stairs, wheezing as they went. Another explosion sounded down below and more caustic soot flooded the escape shaft.

"We're nearly there," Fisher choked.

Lucy felt like she was going to pass out.

Milo pushed an exhausted Thingus up the stairs from behind. Lucy ran down to help, wrapping one of the creature's wings round her shoulder. Fisher followed from a distance, his jaw set.

Laboriously, they made their way up the remaining flight of stairs, which levelled out on to a landing. At the end of the platform was a ladder leading up to an open hatch. Through the smoke, Lucy spotted a patch of sky above them. *Starlight.*

Milo coughed and spat. "How are we gonna get Thingus up the ladder? He's got hooves, not hands."

Lucy tried to lift the beast's front while Milo grabbed his rear, but they had no strength left to lift the creature. Breathing heavily, Thingus's head drooped.

"I'll take it from here." Fisher reached out to pick up the limp being.

Thingus bucked at Fisher's approach, leaping away in terror.

"Thingus," shouted Milo, "you've got wings. Use them!"

Backed against the wall, Thingus hissed fiercely at Fisher and fanned his massive wings. With one last look at Milo with his strange lizard eyes, Thingus flapped with all his might. Making a mighty leap, he tore up through the opening and soared into the air, disappearing into the twinkling night sky.

CHAPTER 23

The End

Milo filled his lungs with the clean, cold orchard air. It was a welcome respite from the pungent smoke that was still pouring out of the open hatchway behind him. He, Lucy and his father had emerged outside the dense grove of trees that concealed the geodesic dome, a dozen yards away from the no-longer-so-secret lab entrance.

Thirty-odd scientists milled around, coughing and wiping their sooty faces with flimsy white jackets. Many were staring in awe at Thingus, who was circling overhead like a griffin. He cackled and cawed, somersaulting through the heavens, exalting in his freedom and his newfound ability to fly.

"We did it," said Milo, exhaling with relief.

"Thanks to you," said Lucy, "Thingus is having as much fun up there as a mosquito at a nude beach." She handed her scarf to Milo.

"Thanks," he smiled.

"We wouldn't want Miss Sladan to catch cold, now would we?" Mr Fisher took the scarf and tossed it back to Lucy, then placed his suit jacket round his son's shoulders.

Milo hugged his father. He began to hope that, in time, Mr Fisher would understand that Thingus wasn't a threat. There was so much they had yet to learn about his species. Maybe Lucy was right, and the Pretenders really were harmless? *Wait, where did she go?*

For a moment Milo was worried she'd headed off without saying goodbye, but he caught sight of her up a nearby tree scarred with harvesting gashes.

"Where are the other Pretenders?" she called down.

Milo presumed she was referring to the magpies and the ibex who had helped Thingus escape. *Huh. Good question.*

A handful of scientists doled out silver-foil blankets to their underdressed colleagues. Milo hoped they had given one to those chimpanzees as well.

"There he is!" a booming voice called out.

Mr Murl ran through the muck towards Mr Fisher, carrying a black tactical jacket under his arm.

Mr Fisher gladly took the coat. "Is the team in position?" he asked.

"Yes, sir," said Murl. "Alpha Six is ready, at your signal."

"Good. Clear out the scientists. I don't want civilians in the area."

"Understood," said Murl. "And the children?"

Fisher paused, pondering.

Surely he won't send me away now? Not after all this.

"Leave them with me," said Fisher, to

Milo's relief. "My son will only benefit from participating in the next phase. And as for the girl, I think it's time we find out how much she really knows."

Murl saluted curtly and hurried off, ordering the scientists to get to their cars and head home.

Lucy climbed down and sloshed back through the mud. "I'm glad Thingus is enjoying his wings, but it's not safe for him to stick around." She cleaned her filthy glasses on her shirt. "Why doesn't he leave?"

"I think he's just happy," said Milo. "Aren't you?"

Lucy grinned. "You know what we need?"

"A mint milkshake," they both said simultaneously, then burst out laughing, the kind of laughter that happens when you're exhausted and relieved and feeling safe at long last after a brain-meltingly stressful day. The kind of laughter that sometimes comes too early.

Out of the corner of his eye Milo saw his father

raise his hand, his fingers splayed. Murl was standing to attention several yards away. *What are they doing now?* Fisher abruptly closed his open fingers into a fist and Murl shouted into his walkie-talkie, "Now!"

A shot rang out from somewhere unseen, loud as a cannon. Lucy flung her hands over her ears while Milo stood frozen and bewildered. Up above, a big and blobby projectile of sap hit Thingus, nearly blacking him out from view. The creature's yowl echoed across the Big Crater Valley, his wings no longer able to keep him aloft, as he fell from an incredible height.

"What are you doing?" Milo ran to his father. "You said you'd let him go."

"I said he'd get to the surface, and I kept my word." Mr Fisher watched as Thingus toppled helplessly towards the far edge of the orchard.

"You've killed him," Milo shrieked.

Fisher grabbed his son by the shoulders and looked him squarely in the eye. "The monster will be fine. Trust me."

"Trust you?" Lucy shouted. "You've done nothing but destroy things since you came here."

Off in the distance, Thingus hit the earth with a horrendous BOOM. A spray of mud shot into the air like a geyser, marking the place he landed. Milo felt sick rise at the back of his throat.

Fisher brusquely signalled to Mr Murl. The head henchman whistled, and twenty armed security operatives zigzagged through the orchard towards the fallen creature.

"Follow me," Fisher shouted to his son as he ran off towards the crash site.

Lucy threw her arms round Milo. "Don't go," she begged. "It's too awful. I don't want you to see..."

Milo's feet and face felt numb. What had his father done? "I have to," he said. He pushed away and walked, zombie-like, towards his friend, surely smashed to a million pieces, just like that. *And for what?*

Lucy was pacing in panicked circles. For a

moment it seemed she couldn't bring herself to follow, but soon enough she chased after Milo and took his hand in hers. "I won't let you go alone."

Milo squeezed Lucy's hand tightly as they approached the impact site, which was completely surrounded by men in uniforms, each standing at military readiness and holding a high-tech weapon. Mr Fisher oversaw the action, standing on the bed of an armoured pickup truck parked at the edge of the orchard. A fleet of drones hovered overhead, directing beams of bright light around the scene. Fresh soil scattered out from the nucleus of the crash where a figure, half buried in the ground, was moving.

Milo's spirit lifted. *He's alive. How?*

Lucy stood on her toes, trying to see. Milo could hear Thingus moaning faintly beneath the throbbing mound of dirt.

"Mmmmrrrrr..." The creature tried to struggle to his feet.

The sound of cocking weaponry clicked round the circle of Fisher's men like the warning of a rattlesnake.

"Mmmmrrrrhhhhhh..." Thingus moaned again, his voice wavering. Soil cascading from his shoulders, the fallen being stood up properly at last. Once again, Thingus had mutated into a hybrid imitation of his human friends. His trembling lips were bowed like Lucy's. His eyes were blue, like Milo's, and filled with tears. "Mmmuh. Mmmilo!" he called in his oscillating, ethereal voice.

"No way," Lucy gasped. "He really is a Pretender, isn't he?"

Other than smears of black sap on his approximated yellow rain gear, Thingus appeared to be miraculously unscathed. "Milo," he cried, reaching out. "Halp!"

Milo started towards him, but the nearest men closed ranks, blocking Thingus from view. "Please, please let Thingus go," he begged his father.

"Not until they show themselves," answered Fisher.

"Who?" said Milo.

"FIRE," barked Murl.

One of the men discharged his weapon and Thingus was hit with a jolt of electricity that coursed over his body in a cobweb of light. Another man fired a shoulder cannon that coated the creature in a thick glob of pink goo.

"NYAAAAAWWWXXX!" screamed Thingus, dropping to the wet earth like a stunned eel, twitching torturously and unable to change form.

"Stop!" Milo hollered.

"That's enough, Fisher!" A woman's voice rang out with all the force of a hurricane.

A silence fell on the field as all the men turned their weapons towards the orchard. The Other Mrs Stricks marched through the trees and out into the open, a few yards from the truck on which Fisher stood. Instead of her customary *muumuu*, she wore a crimson hooded monk-like robe that trailed on the ground behind her. The ibex, which stood as tall as her shoulder, trotted beside her, its head bowed as if poised to charge. The mischievous magpies were perched on each of its imposing horns.

"You've made your point, Richard." The Other Mrs Stricks held her arms out at her sides, her palms open in a gesture of peace. Tufts of frizzy silver hair danced in the wind around her stern face.

Fisher nodded to Murl, who signalled to his men. One by one, they holstered their weapons.

The Other Mrs Stricks snapped her fingers. The magpies fluttered down to the ground, where their small bodies shimmered, expanded and lengthened in a series of airy huffs. The goat jellified, rumbling bulbously until it grew to the height and width of a tall man with a potbelly. The creatures' hair and feathers slithered and stitched themselves into identical flowing red robes. Steve Kozlowski, Kenzo and Marietta Corbin now stood beside the Other Mrs Stricks, glowering at Fisher from beneath their matching hoods.

"Fudgesicles," said Lucy.

Mr Fisher jumped down from the truck and approached them. "I thought we agreed you wouldn't interfere with my operation."

"We did," said the Other Mrs Stricks. "But you neglected to mention that your operation was not very nice." She smiled mockingly. "Now, why don't you do us all a favour and let the kid go?"

Fisher glanced sceptically at Thingus, who was whimpering in the foetal position. "That *kid*, as you call it, is being held as collateral solely because of your irresponsible and hostile acts of sabotage."

"The only thing we sabotaged were your attempts to tear this valley to pieces," shouted Marietta Corbin.

"Not to mention us!" added Kenzo.

"Nu Co. is advancing its interests in compliance with the letter of the law," Fisher retorted, "and we have no intention of stopping now."

"Well then," said the Other Mrs Stricks, "it seems we have something of a chicken and egg problem, don't we?"

Steve Kozlowski advanced towards Fisher, his fists clenched. Kenzo stopped him with a hand to the shoulder.

"It's time for you and your kind to leave this valley," said Fisher.

"That's funny," said the Other Mrs Stricks. "I was going to say the same thing to you."

A look of surprise flashed across Mr Fisher's face. "You don't have a choice," he insisted.

"Is that what you think?" The old woman snapped her fingers again.

ZZZZZBAKKKKCHHOWWW!

With a deafening blast, four bolts of lightning zapped down from the heavens, striking in a circle round the crowded crash site.

Milo ducked, pulling Lucy to the ground along with him.

Spooked, the security forces charged into one another, trying to figure out which way to run. The drones hovering overhead short-circuited in a spray of hot sparks, their spotlights faltering. One by one, they spun hazardously out of control. Some crashed into trees while others simply dropped out of the sky, CHONKing to the ground as frenzied soldiers jumped out of the way.

Lucy leapt over Milo as a drone, its rotor blades still spinning, smacked down in the spot she had lain an instant ago.

"Where did the lightning come from?" said Milo. "There's not a cloud in the sky."

"That's not normal lightning," said Lucy.

The smoke cleared, the bitter scent of burnt metal permeating the area. Four human forms stood in each spot where the bolts had struck, their crimson hoods raised.

Milo strained to see them, slowly realising that each of their faces were familiar. *Carlos Felina. Mrs Stricks. Alastair Chelon. Mandy Millepoids.*

Holy crum. It's all of them. And they can travel through lightning. He swallowed. *Who are these people?*

"Milo!" Fisher called from behind the truck. "Get over here, quickly!"

Without a second thought, Milo obeyed. "Come on," he urged Lucy. Tentatively, she followed.

Mr Fisher lifted the kids on to the heavy-duty truck bed and slammed the tailgate shut. "Stay here," he ordered.

Milo backed against the window of the cab. Lucy watched the scene unfold, a shadow of worry on her face.

The security team had finally sorted themselves into formation, each crouched round the immobilised Thingus, their weapons pointed out at the ring of Pretenders.

"Fisher," Carlos Felina purred, "this is your last chance." The moustachioed weatherman stood four yards away from Milo and Lucy on the other side of the truck. "Release the young one."

Fisher marched to the edge of Thingus's crater, Murl at his side with his stun gun drawn. Milo wondered what his father would do to protect his men. What were these creatures, and what were they capable of?

"He'd better not hurt Thingus again," Lucy hissed through her teeth.

Milo was struggling to wrap his brain round it all. Who was in the right? "The Pretenders need to back down," he said. "They're only making it worse."

Lucy scowled. "Your dad's goons are the ones who should back down."

"The Pretenders shouldn't have broken my father's machines."

"Your dad shouldn't have kidnapped Thingus," she snapped.

"No," Milo agreed. "He shouldn't." Lucy was right. What his father had done was wrong, but Milo knew he thought he was doing it for the right reasons. *It's never okay to hurt anyone. Is it?*

"We simply want things to return to they way

they were, Fisher," declared Mandy Millepoids, his tall silhouette clearly visible on the far side of the circle. "Don't be a fool."

"If you refuse to go, Richard," said Mrs Stricks from across the way, "we cannot be held responsible for the fate that befalls you."

Fisher turned to his companion. "Ready, Mr Murl."

Murl pointed his weapon at Thingus, preparing to fire.

Milo felt like he might faint. *Don't do it, Dad. Please.*

"All right," said the Other Mrs Stricks. "Have it your way." She snapped her fingers once more.

Each of the Pretenders' eyes began to glow fiery orange.

What the—

"Agghh!" Murl threw his taser to the ground. "It's hot!"

Squealing in turn, all the security operatives tossed their guns away, waving their scorched, steaming hands as their weapons sparked and fizzled in the mud, affected by some unseen force unleashed by the paranormal creatures around them.

"What is this?" said Fisher, looking around in alarm.

Another boom rang out as a bolt of lightning shot down from the clear sky and struck Thingus, who vanished in a burst of sound and smoke. Murl and Fisher were thrown by the force of the blast, colliding violently with the men around them.

"Dad!" Milo watched his father stagger to his feet.

A low hum emanated throughout the clearing as the Pretenders chanted in unison in an unrecognisable tongue, their eyes shining brighter and brighter in a dynamic spectrum of colour, turning yellow, then blue, then violet. The ground began to shake.

"What's happening?" Milo asked.

For once Lucy didn't have an answer. She gripped the truck's tailgate, fear in her eyes.

The truck jolted and Milo fell painfully to his knees. A puff of smoke burst from under the hood as the motor overheated, presumably caused by the same force that had felled the drones and the high-tech weaponry. Milo had never dreamed that such terrifying power was possible.

He scanned the chaotic scene of prostrate security men. His father was standing at the centre of it all, looking remarkably unconcerned. In fact, he was laughing.

"Dad, you have to get out of there!" Milo yelled.

Mr Fisher reached into his pocket and pulled out a walkie-talkie. "Unit Two," he commanded, "let's show them what we've got. Go!"

BANG! BANG! BANG! BANG! BANG! BANG! BANG! BANG! BANG! BANG!

Shot after ear-splitting shot was fired as the Pretenders were peppered with large syringe-like darts filled with a shimmering sky-blue liquid. *Substance Nu-791*. Howling in pain and fear, their eyes stopped glowing and the earth's shaking subsided.

Milo peered over at Carlos Felina. Or what was left of him. The floundering weatherman, three yards away and covered in darts, no longer appeared human. His shape stretched and sagged. His skin glowed like the moonlight. It almost looked like he was melting, except he was growing larger instead.

The wails of the Pretenders echoed around the orchard, as each of them morphed hideously into an endless array of unearthly forms. Two giant beasts made of glimmering goo lumbered towards one other – was it Kenzo and Marietta Corbin? They collided in a twisted embrace, their bodies fusing together, their swollen, misshapen mouths howling piteously at either side.

Mr Fisher gazed upon his handiwork with excited uncertainty.

Dad, what have you done? thought Milo.

The unnerved security squad gaped at the scene around them. One of the men vomited in the mud.

"Get the nets!" Mr Fisher shouted into his walkie-talkie. He jogged over to the pickup truck.

"It's over," said Fisher. "The two of you need to get back home befo—" He lurched forward as the ground shook violently once again.

Milo and Lucy clung to one another to keep from falling.

Fisher scrambled to his feet, unsteady as the quakes continued. "It's not possible. How?"

Milo became aware of a strange cicada-like chittering rising from the forest across the clearing. He whipped round. There, rising up through the trees in a wave of fluttering sound that washed over the sky, were eyes. Dozens of violet glowing eyes.

Lucy started to laugh, although Milo wasn't sure what was funny.

"He thought the Pretenders were all people." She seemed hardly able to catch her breath. "But why would they be?"

"What do you mean?" snapped Mr Fisher.

Milo understood. "It's the animals," he said. "Some of the animals are Pretenders, too." *Of course.* Not all the members of this race chose a human form. Why not remain a rabbit, or a raccoon, or an owl if you had the option? Perhaps, to them, humanity was overrated.

Fisher's wan expression made him seem older than his forty-odd years.

The luminous creatures swirled overhead in a sonorous swarm. Sharply, the amplitude of the tremors increased and Lucy was thrown from the truck. Milo leapt down after her just as, with a tremendous CRACKKKKKKKKKK, the ground split and broke open. The smell of sulphur gusted out of the fissure.

The rift sped through the orchard, encompassing the grove at the centre. "No," cried Fisher as he heard the geodesic dome buckle and crumble.

A blast of lightning struck once more as blinding bolts rained down, striking each of the eight humanoid Pretenders. When the smoke cleared, all of the suffering gelatinous beings had disappeared, leaving nothing but puffs of smoke in their wake.

The chasm widened, trees toppling into its depths. In seconds it swallowed the dome in a crunch of twisted metal beams. Fisher's security ops escaped into the forest and clambered over the chain-link fence in mortal desperation.

Following the structural line of the underground tunnel, the crack in the earth continued its rapid spread towards the Nu Co. factory.

"No!" Fisher bolted towards the massive brick building, like a child trying to catch a glass vase before it shattered on the floor.

"He's crazy," said Lucy.

His heart beating out of his chest, Milo took off after his father.

"Careful!" cried Lucy. She raced over and pulled him back as the void widened again, nearly reaching Milo's feet. They teetered on the edge as more trees plunged into its fathomless depths, crashing against the crumbling wreckage of the underground laboratory.

Giving the ever-expanding fissure a wide berth, Milo and Lucy ran towards the factory. When they reached the employee parking lot, they found Fisher standing on the roof of his silver sedan, swinging his fist at the sky.

An expansive murmuration of sparkling violet roiled above the brick building, the many unnatural birds and bats shrieking cacophonously.

The parking lot broke open, consuming a handful of cars and trucks as the chasm split and encircled the factory.

Fisher ran towards the building, his eyes wild.

"It's going to collapse," Lucy warned.

With a hideous creaking wail the pyramidal smokestack began to judder and sway, bricks breaking free and toppling down its sides. The mossy base of the complex began to crumble, and then, all at once and with a terrifying groan, the structure caved in, its parts cascading into the hot bowels of the Earth.

Fisher tripped frantically across the shattered pavement to the edge of the gaping pit, where he fell to his knees in anguish. With one final rumble, the shrill animal murmur ceased and the orchestra of glowing eyes extinguished themselves. At last, the tremors slowed to a standstill.

The night was engulfed in total silence.

"Gone," said Fisher.

Milo hadn't seen his father look so powerless since the day his mother had died.

"Come on, Dad." Milo beckoned from beside the sedan. "Please."

"Nu Co." Fisher stood. "It's all gone."

"I'm still here," said Milo. He held out his hand.

Jerking himself out of a daze, Fisher took a step towards his son, but the ground crumbled under his feet. "W-whoa," he waved his arms to keep his balance but it was too late. He was falling into the hole.

Milo's senses dulled as he dashed to save his father, like he was running in slow motion through a tunnel of fog. Fisher clawed at the edge of the disintegrating cliff, his nails scratching against the asphalt, grappling to hold on.

Milo slid out on his knees and caught his father's hand, but he wasn't strong enough – they were both being pulled into the abyss. "Come on, Dad, climb!"

Fisher struggled to find a foothold on the sheer rock face. "Let go," Fisher ordered his son.

"Never!" Milo strained to tighten his grasp. He could feel his father slipping away. Then another pair of hands gripped Fisher's flailing arm. Milo looked over to see Lucy, beet-red, pulling his father up with all her might.

Lucy and Milo heaved in tandem. Slowly, slowly, they lifted Mr Fisher out of the crumbling hole and dragged him into the parking lot, where he collapsed on the solid ground.

Lucy rested against the wheel of Fisher's sedan, panting. She gave Milo a thumbs-up, then closed her eyes tightly.

Milo lay on his back, staring into a star-studded sky that seemed to be spinning. They were safe. But for how long? Both Lucy and his father had been right. The world was not as simple as it seemed. And now Milo knew something that even Lucy had to agree with.

Sticky Pines is full of monsters. The Pretenders must be stopped, before it's too late.

CHAPTER 24

Fisher's Fissure

"Mr Fisher is a monster." Lucy's tongue poked out the side of her mouth as she typed up the article for the *SPEAMS Sentinel* on her battered laptop. *Gertie's mind is about to be so blown her nose ring might fly off. Maybe* I'll *be the one to get that scholarship to Stanford, after I win a Pulitzer and get elected leader of the solar system.*

Lucy typed at the coffee table in the living room, knees drawn up to her chin, the warmth of the wood-burning stove at her back. She was only vaguely distracted by the clinking of dishes being washed in the kitchen and Willow's squeaks of glee each time she fitted a jigsaw-puzzle piece. Her father was on the phone in the bedroom, as he had been all afternoon, most likely discussing the fact that nearly everyone he knew had to find a new job.

It had been two days since the demolition of the Nu Co. factory, and Lucy was still sparking with adrenaline. Every corner of the Big Crater Valley had felt the tremors. School was cancelled for the rest of the week and many businesses were closed (including, unsurprisingly, Mandy's Candies and The Woo Woo Store). The whole town was stunned to learn about the factory's demise, but so far Mr Fisher had successfully kept the cause under wraps. Remarkably, it seemed that nobody in his security team had leaked the story to the press. Lucy had overheard her father telling her mother that Mr Fisher had introduced "one heck of a non-disclosure agreement" in everyone's employment contract.

For the first time in Lucy's life the world was totally primed for her to spill all the beans she had, and fast. She'd been working all day to ensure that she'd finish her article before someone tried to convince her to keep quiet. But Lucy was done with lies once and for all. *Eat slugs, secret-mongers!*

She rubbed the dryness out of her eyes and typed on:

As the Nu Co. factory kerplooied into the crater, Mr Fisher's angry purple face looked like it was about to explode into a zillion pieces. He fought like a badger and lost, and Nu Co., as we know it, is no more. Once again, the mysterious Pretenders of Sticky Pines had escaped Fisher's Nucralose of Doom. But though the lives of countless shapeshifting weirdos had been saved, the factory was dustified beyond repair.

There's still tons left to learn about these incredible beings. Who are they? What do they want? Where did they come from? What are their powers? And do they really like candy as much as it seems? But two undeniable TRUTHS remain: one, many of our friends and neighbours (and possibly pets?) are actually extranatural transmutational beings of unknown origin;

and, two, by playing with forces he doesn't understand, Mr Fisher is putting Sticky Pines, and possibly the whole world, at risk. He must be stopped, before it's too late.

That's it. She smacked her hands. *It's ready.* She attached the document to an email – subject line: "FRONT-PAGE BONANZA" – and sent it off to Gertie Lee.

"Why do you look so triumphant?" said Miranda Sladan, watching her daughter from behind the kitchen island. "You're still grounded, you know."

"I know," Lucy sang. *But not for long.* She was pretty sure that making the front page of every single newspaper in the universe would counteract the trouble she was in for getting home "later than your father or I thought possible to even dream".

Following the undeniable and irreversible destruction of the Nu Co. factory, Mr Fisher had unceremoniously dropped off Lucy, her bike and the metric ton of dust they were covered in at the end of her driveway. He'd driven off without a word. Lucy was pretty sure he'd only offered her the ride in the first place because she'd helped save his life. It seemed a fair enough trade.

Lucy's parents had greeted her at the door with equal parts anger and relief. They'd asked her where she'd been and if she had felt the earthquake. Lucy had intended to tell them everything that had happened, but she'd started with, "I saw the Nu Co. factory fall into a giant hole in the ground," and the conversation quickly got out of hand. Her statement seemed to confirm a rumour her parents had heard, which sent them into an increasingly upsetting series of phone calls. After that, Lucy decided it might be best for them to read about what really happened on the front page of the school paper before the onslaught of TV interviews began.

She checked her messages. There was one from Milo: "Did you finish the article?"

Lucy typed a response: "i just hit send."

Three dots appeared in the message window as Milo wrote back. "Did you tell the Whole Truth?"

"i put in EVERYTHING. start to finish. top to bottom. creatures to catastrophes :-O"

":-O Good."

"wanna meet up at Buck's tomorrow?"

"I would, but my dad and I are heading up to Vancouver for a couple days. We can grab a shake when I get back!"

"deal."

":-)"

":-D"

Willow jumped to her feet. "I've done it," she beamed. "This is the last piece." She inserted it into the puzzle dramatically. "Ta-dah!"

Lucy leaned over and examined the jigsaw, a near complete print of "The Starry Night" by Vincent Van Gogh. "There's still a piece missing, Will."

"What?" Willow bent down to look. There was indeed, another empty space on the board. She fell back on to the couch, sinking into its deep cushions. "Oh."

"Check under the rug," Lucy hopped over a sleeping Errol and sauntered into the kitchen. "'Sup, *señorita,*" she said to her mother. She grabbed an apple from the fruit bowl.

Miranda scrutinised her sassy daughter as she dried the soup pot. "Did you finish your article?"

"Did I ever." Lucy plopped down on a stool, chewing loudly.

"You've been so secretive about it. What angle did you take?"

Errol trotted into the kitchen and stared hopefully up at Lucy. She bit off a piece of the apple and tossed it into his open mouth.

"Well," said Lucy, "I can't tell you what it's about, but I can tell you the title."

Miranda stuffed the pot into the cupboard. "I'm all ears, maestro."

Lucy placed each word on an imaginary banner with her hand. "Monsters, Madness and Machinations: The Mysteries of Sticky Pines Revealed."

"That sounds very exciting. But I thought you were writing about Nu Co., not the supernatural." Miranda wiped down the counter. "You could have written about the earthquake. Isn't that enough excitement for you?"

"Everything is connected," Lucy winked.

Miranda tossed the towel on the counter, clearly concerned for her daughter's psychological well-being.

Silas shuffled into the room wearing his coat and boots. "I'm heading off to the Banana Slug Saloon. Some of the guys are there, commiserating. There's a lot to discuss."

"Understatement of the millennium," Miranda sighed.

"Will Alastair Chelon be there?" asked Lucy.

"I dunno." Silas hugged Lucy and smoothed her bushy hair. "I haven't heard from him today." He froze halfway to the door. "Gosh, I hope he's okay. They did say the factory was empty when it went down, didn't they?"

"He's fine, don't worry." Lucy waved off his concern.

"How would you—" Silas was cut short when Willow ran up and clung to his legs from behind. He caught himself on the counter and pulled her up into a koala bear hug. "I've gotta run, kiddette." He kissed her forehead. "I'll see you in the morning. But not too early!" He set her down on the peeling linoleum floor.

Lucy's parents shared a solemn gaze before Silas stepped out into the garage.

"Is Dad gonna be okay?" Willow asked once the door had closed behind him. "Without a job, I mean."

Lucy scoffed. "He *hated* that job, especially since Fisher took over. He'll find a new one, easy. Right, Mom?"

Miranda nodded stiffly. "We'll be fine, girls. Don't worry." She went into the living room and switched on the television, turning the volume up high.

The phone rang. Lucy reached for the cordless

receiver on the wall but Willow got to it first.

"H'lo?" she said. "No, *you're* a silly goose."

Lucy could hear the sound of laughter on the other line. "Who are you talking to?"

"It's for you." Willow handed her the phone.

"Lucille," said Tex. "When did you become a comic genius?"

"Since birth," she replied. "Why?"

"We just read your piece for the paper. We have not laughed so much in ages."

Lucy heard a female voice giggling in the background. "We?"

"Gertie is here," said Tex.

What?

"In light of the unanticipated school closure," he continued, "I have graciously offered Ms Lee the use of my processing power to ensure that the *Sentinel* is printed on time."

Has the apocalypse begun?

"Sladan." Gertie took the phone. "You're amazing. This piece would go great in the satire section, if we had a satire section, which we don't. Where's the real article?"

"The, uh –" Lucy lowered her voice so her mother wouldn't hear – "real article? That is the article. Every word is true."

There was silence on the other line. Errol whimpered for more apple. Lucy gave him the rest of her half-eaten piece of fruit. For a moment the phone seemed to have gone dead. Had Gertie put her on mute?

"Right," Gertie said at last. "Listen, I'm gonna be straight with you. We can't use any of this. I told you from the start I was interested in the Truth, not some made-up mumbo jumbo. It's a fun story. A secret underground lair, mad scientists, our English teacher's wife as the ringleader of an inhuman species of shapeshifters. You should consider submitting it to the annual fiction anthology. I bet Mrs Stricks'd get a kick out of it."

Lucy's knees felt weak.

Willow chased Errol across the floor, then stopped to stare at her big sister, who was looking paler by the second. "What's wrong?" she mouthed.

"But it's the Truth, Gertie," said Lucy. "I swear. How else do you think the factory got destroyed?"

"Oh, *that* mystery's been solved. Did you know that fracking can cause earthquakes?"

"Fracking? Like, breaking the ground open to get oil?"

"That's right," said Gertie. "Word on the mycelium network is there's a whole mess of it under Sticky Pines. That explains why they're still tearing down the forest despite not producing any Nucralose. Oil's what Fisher's really after."

"What is this network you keep mentioning?" Lucy asked.

"It was on the news."

Lucy leaned over the island to see the TV. Her mother was watching tensely as a female news anchor wearing a truckload of make-up interviewed Mr Fisher. The words "Fracking

Accident Destroys Nu Co. Plant" scrolled across the bottom of the screen. Lucy's jaw fell open. *No.*

"These big-city oil-mongers think they can get away with tearing small towns apart with no consequences," Gertie proclaimed loudly in Lucy's ear. "Causing explosions, earthquakes and spill after greasy spill. Well, not on our watch!" Lucy pictured Gertie standing on a chair in Tex's kitchen. "The climate crisis must be addressed, not in a year, not in a week, but TODAY—" And then, in muffled tones: "That's good, get that down, Arkhipov. There's our front-page op-ed."

Lucy heard Tex typing in the background. "The truth must out!" he shouted.

"Sorry it didn't work out, Sladan," said Gertie. "I'll, uh, see you when I see you." She hung up.

Lucy stared at the phone. *What just happened?* This was it. The best chance she'd ever had to get the Truth out to the world, and somehow she'd been foiled again.

"*I* believe you," said Willow. She handed Lucy half the clementine she'd just peeled.

"Huh?" said Lucy, slumping on to the stool. She hung up the phone and looked at the small orange in her hand as if unsure what it was. "You didn't even read the article I wrote."

"Doesn't matter." Willow crossed her arms. "You're my sister and I believe whatever you believe. Even if it's dumb."

Lucy smiled ruefully. "Thanks, Will." She ruffled Willow's fringe, then joined her mother in the living room.

"I can't believe this is happening," said Miranda, staring at the news broadcast in shock. "I thought that factory would be around forever. Everyone did." She held her face in her palms. "Just when you think you've got a handle on things..."

"Something comes along and pulls the rug out from under you," said Lucy.

Miranda took her daughter's hand, not caring that it was sticky with clementine juice. "I don't want you to worry, okay? This is a very big challenge for us, but everything will feel normal again before you know it."

"Thanks, Mom." Lucy spotted something sticking halfway out from under the couch: Willow's missing puzzle piece. She picked it up and plugged it into the last slot of the jigsaw on the coffee table. "We'll figure it out."

The Nu Co. disaster site was cordoned off with police tape and surrounded by fire trucks with red and blue lights flashing. A team of men in yellow hazmat suits combed the area with detectors that clicked and beeped. Wisps of smoke rose from the depths of the open chasm, which was now ringed by heavy cranes dangling long metal winches into its bowels.

"Salvage anything you can," Murl barked into a loudspeaker. He stood on the steps of a mobile office parked on the remnants of what was once Nu Co.'s parking lot. "Leave no rock unturned."

"Are you sure we can't use any of my officers?"

asked Sheriff Pryce, her hazmat suit tucked untidily into her cowboy boots. "They know this area better'n anybody."

"There's no need for police presence, ma'am," Murl assured her, the low sun glinting off his aviator sunglasses. "Fracking materials are highly hazardous, and the ground remains unstable. Best leave it to the private sector."

The sheriff leaned against the railing. "Fracking," she grouched. "I thought this was a sweetener operation, pure and simple. Why on the round blue Earth were you going underground?"

"I'm sure Mr Fisher's got all the relevant paperwork," Murl responded.

"We'll be seein' about that." Sheriff Pryce stormed off to her patrol car at the base of the Nu Co. driveway.

Murl sniffed. "At least the orchard's toast," he muttered to himself. "We'll be leaving this ramshackle village of freaks once and for all." There was a crackle and a distorted voice sounded from the satchel at Murl's side. "Sir?"

Murl retrieved his walkie-talkie. "I copy, Fandango. What's up?"

"Sir, there's something down here I think you're gonna want to see."

Ugh. "Copy that." Murl tucked away the walkie-talkie. "This place," he grumbled, as he marched through a pathway littered with broken branches and sharp, twisted stumps.

He reached the team working the crane, and with their assistance he strapped himself securely into a harness. A pair of men, their faces obscured by hard hats and breathing masks, attached him to the hook on the crane's lead, then lowered him into the smouldering ravine.

The darkness of the cavern engulfed him. Murl switched on the torchlight at his shoulder. The journey down took nearly a half an hour, as he was gently lowered past twisted metal girders and sparkling valueless rock formations. By the time he reached the bottom of the pit, he was livid.

"This better be good," he growled as his feet found solid yellow rock. Behind him on the ruined cavern wall were the last vestiges of stupid child-like carvings of deer and chickens with some nonsense symbols thrown in. "Didn't even have a podcast to listen to..." he grumbled. "No reception..."

A scientist in protective gear ran up to him excitedly. "It's over there, sir." He pointed to an area where five workers were bent over, examining a narrow chasm in the floor with torches. "We're not sure what it is, but it could be something big."

Murl brushed past him. He joined the others and knelt on the ground, directing his torchlight downwards. He stopped short. *Unbelievable.* "That better not be what I think it is."

"I've got a sample of it right here." A woman held out a beaker filled with a dense syrupy liquid.

Murl's face fell. He stuck a finger into the beaker and let the gloppy black substance run over his glove, like glue.

Son of a… Murl glowered as he peered into the accursed cleft. There was no way around it – he'd have to tell Fisher. And once he did, Nu Co. would not be going anywhere after all. For flowing beneath his feet was a vast river of something dark, thick, and very, very sticky.

ACKNOWLEDGEMENTS

I offer my sincerest thanks to the following: my savvy and stylish agent Laura West; my editors Maurice Lyon and Kirsty Stansfield; the team at Nosy Crow, whether working from home during quarantine or at the Crow's Nest; my brilliant cover illustrator Bill Bragg; my first fan and earliest reader Anna Tullis; my fabulous friends and indispensable cultural liaisons Asya and Paul Mourraille and Spooky Ruño; the Swaggers – an oasis of good prose and saucy GIFs in a mad, mad world; my mother Maribeth and brother Jesse for their enthusiastic support of all things Sticky Pines; Monkey, my constant companion and guiding light into the unknown; and, of course, JGR, without whose warm dedication, unsparing assistance, and late night semantic debatery this book would not exist.

Find out how it all started in

CHAPTER 1

Encounter of a Weird Kind

After all the times she had insisted that something was out there, after all the times no one believed her, after the lifetime of sniggering she had endured – tonight, Lucy Sladan would prove she was right.

With a CLICK, she loaded a roll of film into the old camera she had "borrowed" from her parents. She needed proof, the kind that was hard to fake. *People of the world*, she thought, *prepare to learn the Truth*.

Her skin tingled with excitement. She still couldn't quite believe it. Just the night before, while taking the dog out for a gallop in the woods,

Lucy had seen something in the sky; something that looked remarkably, amazingly, like the out-of-focus flying objects pictured on her favourite website: *TheTruthHasLanded.org*.

A flash of lightning outside the round attic window cast jagged shadows across the sloped walls. For a fleeting moment, Lucy's bedroom seemed full of motion. She twisted a lock of purple hair and counted out six Mississippis before she heard the corresponding rumble of thunder. Pushing her plastic-framed glasses up the bridge of her nose, she reread a highlighted article in yesterday's newspaper:

SECOND DISAPPEARANCE IN STICKY PINES

Beloved candy-store owner, Mandy Millepoids, 66, has been reported missing. He was last seen birdwatching in Molasses Grove on the evening of September 1. Meanwhile, police are still searching for factory worker Alastair Chelon, 37, last seen fishing at Black Hole Lake on August 17. Authorities are looking into sightings of large wild animals in the area.

Wild animals, Lucy scoffed. She knew the truth. *These guys weren't attacked. They were abducted. By ALIENS.*

She imagined the article they would write about her tomorrow: *Lucy Sladan, 12-year-old genius, rescues missing Sticky Pines residents while awesomely confirming once and for all the existence of extraterrestrials. Former critics are amazed and deeply apologetic.*

All she needed to do now was sneak out without getting caught.

A knock on the door sent the newspaper flying out of her hands in a dozen fluttering pieces. Her nine-year-old sister Willow entered without waiting for an invitation. Lucy wondered why she bothered to hang the "Keep Out, Unbelievers" sign on the door.

"What are you doing up here?" asked Willow. "Listening for radio signals from space?"

"Too much cloud cover." Lucy glanced at the clipping from *The ET Bee* pinned to the corkboard above her desk. The headline read:

"Do Aliens Use Bad Weather to Hide from Sight?" Lucy knew the answer: *You bet they flippin' do.* She gathered up the newspaper and put it back together in no particular order. "I think I'm gonna hit the hay early tonight."

"Your bedtime's not for two hours," said Willow.

"What can I say?" Lucy stretched her arms and yawned, fairly convincingly. "I'm bushed."

"You're not in your pyjamas."

"I was ... just about to change." *Keep it together, Lucita. Sneaking out is all in the details.* She had googled it.

Willow kicked a pile of dirty clothes and hopped over to sit on the rumpled bed. "Did you hear there was another Bigfoot sighting?" She chewed the strings of her pink unicorn hoodie. "Dad says Sasquatches only eat boys, but Mom says they're equal opportunity."

Lucy snorted. "Please. Only babies and tourists believe in dumb stuff like Bigfoot."

"You believe in fairies," Willow sneered.

"I believe in transdimensional beings who've been MISTAKEN for fairies."

"Whatever." Willow rolled her eyes. "Errol ran off after dinner again. You're not supposed to feed him people food."

"Eating only dog food is boring, Will." Lucy checked the clock. "Did you want something?"

"Mom and Dad wanna know if you're gonna come make up songs with us," said Willow.

Three nights in a row? "Thanks for the invite, but like I said, I'm bushed."

"It's only eight o'clock," Willow complained. "What are you, five?" She picked up a toy Yoda from the bookshelf and started messing with its ears.

Lucy snatched the precious Jedi out of her hands. "OK, time to go."

"I wasn't gonna break your doll."

"Figurine," Lucy corrected. She scooted her sister out to the golden pine landing. "Tell Mom and Dad not to wake me up. It's a school night."

"Fine." Willow stuck out her tongue and,

mercifully, headed downstairs.

Lucy turned off all the lights and got into bed fully clothed. She stared impatiently into darkness until it was well past Willow's nine o'clock bedtime. Nobody came upstairs to check on her. *It's time.*

TO BE CONTINUED...